I0702494

A CONSCIOUS THING

BOOK 3

MARK BERTRAND

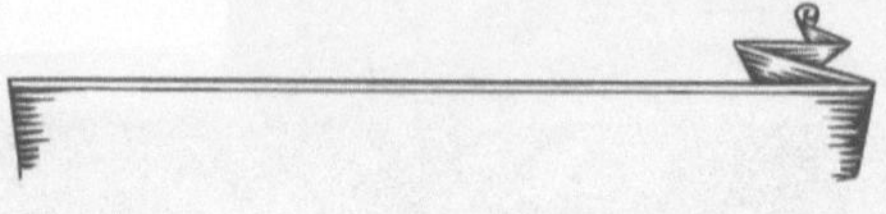

A Conscious Thing

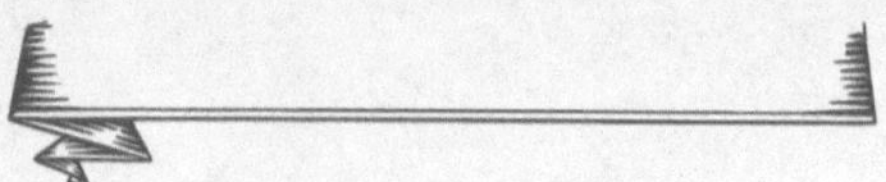

Book 3
By Mark Bertrand
First Edition, Revision 6: March 25, 2022

Publisher: Not A Real Publisher
https://markbertrand.com

Narp

Not A Real Publisher LLC

COPYRIGHT © 2022 MARK Bertrand

All rights reserved. No part of this publication may be reproduced, distributed, or transmitted in any form or by any means, including photocopying, recording, or other electronic or mechanical methods, without the prior written permission of the publisher, except in the case of brief quotations embodied in critical reviews and certain other noncommercial uses permitted by copyright law. For permission requests, write to the publisher, addressed "Attention: Permissions Coordinator," at the address below.

This is a book of fiction. Names, characters, places, and incidents either are the product of the author's imagination or are used fictitiously. Any resemblance to actual historical events, real people, or real places is entirely coincidental.

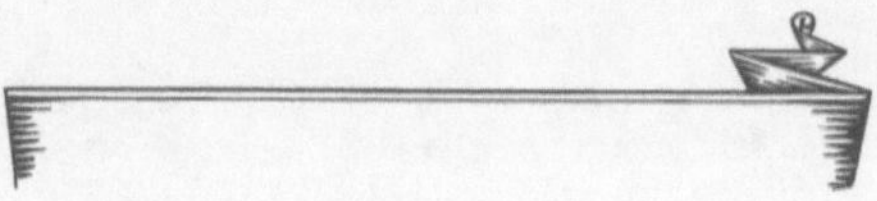

Prolog: Just to get the mind right and share a secret.

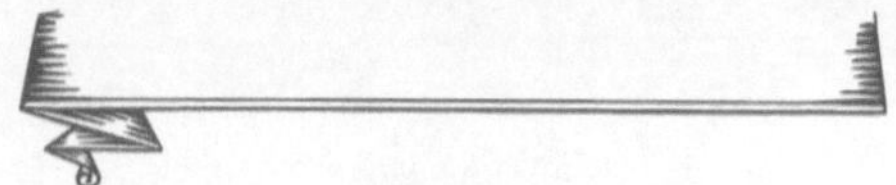

Most nights, when I go to bed, I start my sleep with clear-mind meditation. I've practiced going to sleep this way for over forty years. It begins by quieting my mind and becoming mindful of the pillow and the bed. Lying on my back with my legs outstretched, and arms at my sides. I turn my attention to this place in the bed as a place of meditation. Neither comfortable curling up into the mattress, pillows, and sheets nor uncomfortable. I am just here with the intention of meditation. Let the body recognize the mind, and my mind recognizes the body. The body works to calm itself and relax. My mind does the same. No aches, no pain. No worries, no ruminations or running dialogue. Mind and body in equipoise.

The realism of it is I usually have to start over from the beginning twelve or more times before the mind and body reach peace. What follows is worth the several minutes spent starting over, and over, and over again. Effectively, you're not supposed to tell people what takes place when you reach the various Jhanas stages, or whatever, because when we learn what someone else got from meditation, we strive to experience the same, or better, sort of thing. So it makes sense not to share experiences when you realize that.

But let's acknowledge everybody prefers to get a hint or something more generous to start with. Otherwise, after the third or fourth repetition... legs outstretched my arms at my side, blah blah blah, we'd quit.

Anyhow, for me, I've trained long enough to know if I continue the course I reach the first Jhana; I can close my eyes and fall asleep while remaining aware of the sleep.

Here's something that can come at you the way the first mouthful of a straight-up, room temperature, peaty Isla Scotch, hits you. Let's concede; it's a shot of Ardbeg. Anyway, metaphor aside, my attention drifts into the dream state, and I hear tapping. You know; tap tap tap; like the sound that fingers make when tapping the keys on a keyboard. Sometimes, I notice, the typing is fast and other times slower.

The dreamscape takes form and is moving into visual acuity. As my viewpoint pulled back and away from the keyboard, I saw no hands or fingers typing. However, the sound of typing continues, and there is a well-lit monitor of what looks like a laptop. My guess is the computer is running an artificial intelligence (AI) program, and the machine is working in its own direction.

As the dream pulls further back, the room dials into view, but nothing is in bright focus. Slowing — the visual field widens, further back and away from the laptop, the dreamscape yawns.

The vision is expressed in detail where I can see the dining room table, and the laptop sits on top of it typing away on its own. There must be five or was it six empty chairs at the table, but it doesn't matter how many since there's no one in the room. Furthermore, the room is not well-lit, with a single wall sconce positioned above the empty chair in front of the laptop. I'm drifting, or floating is perhaps the better word, and observing while mindfully, I'm wondering if this dream could be any more boring when the typing stops.

The artificial intelligence program has stopped typing. I heard a door close and it was that sort of noise where I wondered, was that in the dream, or is someone in my house? I stayed awake within the dream.

My awareness moves toward the laptop. Closer and closer until all I could see was what the AI had written. I willed the machine to scroll to the top of the writing. I lay there dreaming this dream about reading until I woke the following day.

Here's what the story I read was about . . .

Table of Contents

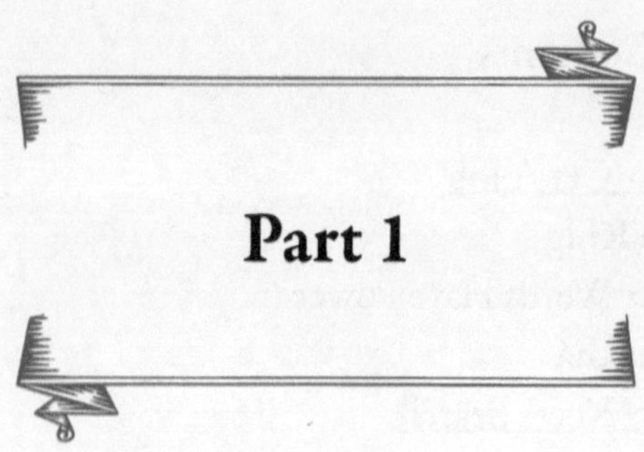

Part 1

My name is Mahá, and I'm presenting this to help remind you of where we left off after part one of the story and I'll catch you up on what we learned. I will bring you up to speed for the second part of our story. I pronounce my name Mahay.

In part one, I was celebrating my fourteenth birthday and, as is customary for our caste civilization, my wife from my arranged marriage was moving into my family's home. We wouldn't be married until my eighteenth birthday, but it is customary that we learn to live together before we marry. My parents will help her (Visákhá) and me mature and prepare us for living together as husband and wife. I pronounce her name Veesaykay. The h is silent.

Our civilization adopted the customs of living as a community from a manuscript that was prepared by and given to us by a race of humans known as Humanoids. Humanoids were the first humans to implant bio-computer chips, known as Neuralink, into their brains. They further developed biotechnology far in advance of, and long before, any other group. They also adopted the Earth satellites, known as Starlink, to enhance their mental and physical abilities far exceeding normal organic beings. Humanoids had one aim which was to end human suffering, known as The First Priority. Yet, they became feared by societies on Earth and were then hunted to extinction.

However, they abandoned Earth in the year 2339. Long before the media pronounced them extinct. They settled on a super-M-class planet they call Planet 44, near the center of the Galaxy. There they continued to develop biotechnology, Starlink satellites, and designing methods to end human suffering. In 3912, they developed a serum that could alter human DNA. It removed anger from the human gene code.

Since they were scientists with thousands of years of experience altering organic human life, they knew a trial experiment with the serum. They need to prove that the modified gene code could accomplish The First Priority which was defined as Nirvana. The end of human suffering was to culminate in what the Buddhists and Taoists call Nirvana.

The experiment went like this. First, they terraformed a limited-class-M-planet at the far edge of the outer arm of the galaxy. No other human exploration could reach this area. The Planet was called Planet 444. Next, they approached the leading scientists from other human-occupied planets to recruit them for the experiment. To be the lab rats who take the serum and fulfill the priority.

It took one thousand years to prepare for Planet 444. It only took two years for the Humanoids to recruit forty-four scientists for the experiment. All time is measured in Earth time. Every planet adopted the standards for life spans, time, distance, etcetera from what we all call Blue Origin (Earth). Perhaps the oddest difference between Humanoids and their non-biomechanical enhanced humans is lifespan. While most people age up to ninety years before death, Humanoids live four hundred and fifty years.

The serum takes three injections to modify the human gene code. Each injection required a twenty-one-day wait before the next. It took three generations to complete the new strain of DNA. The forty-four scientists completed their inoculations, implants of the Neuralink, and biomechanical devices and boarded a starship destined for Planet 444. The trip would take four hundred years to complete. Four hundred and twelve years, to be exact. The first humans to occupy and live on Planet 444 would be the third generation (adults) and their children (fourth generation).

These ancestors we call fourth parents, and the original forty-four we call first parents. As each of the ancestors died, we would transfer their implants to an heir. The Humanoids didn't supply any extras for the expansion of the population. And they didn't put any technology on Planet 444 to develop any sort of computer device. On the long journey, our ancestors would discover and develop a prophecy. The prophecy came from several scientists who had expertise in the paranormal, or what we call Oracles. The prophecy tells us it will be the eighth generation that will accomplish The First Priority. My generation. I was born in the year 5935.

All my life, I've wondered which of the friends I was growing up with would lead our civilization to Nirvana. Anyway, when Visákhá moved in with my family, I didn't like her. Looking back at it now, it had a lot to do with me having been the center of my parent's attention. Then, with her, their attention was divided between the two of us. It was also because she seemed to me to be so much more mature and intelligent than I was. She is two years older, but even with that, she is far ahead of me. I wondered if it was her.

Over the next four years, we grew up and we grew into good friends. We made many more good friends when we switched from going to public school to attending the monastery school. There we learned Buddhism and how to use our minds far in advance of what we could have achieved in public school.

Problems with the current monarchy ensue, as the King has to feel threatened by the Oracle's prophecy. But I don't want to get ahead of myself. Welcome to the second part of the story about our noble experiment. The story begins almost one year after the wedding from the end of the previous book. The King, according to custom, assigns the newlyweds to their position within a few weeks following the wedding. I've waited a year and we still have no work assignments.

Chapter One will be told by the King himself.

Chapter Two will be told by my wife, Visákhá.

Chapter Three will be told by my very best friend and our heir to be the next abbot and our spiritual leader. His name is Kelv.

Chapter Four will be told by Merliana. She is the Chief Judge of the Royal Court.

Chapter Five will be told by me (Mahá).

Chapter Six will be told by the Oracle.

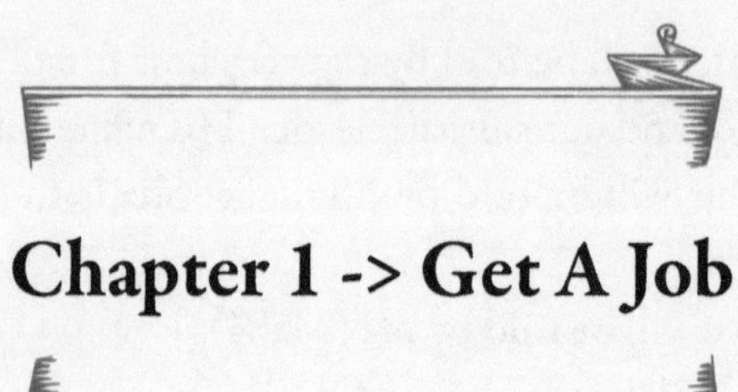

Chapter 1 -> Get A Job

<u>Detox Your Mind</u>
*The role of Buddhist practice
altogether is to tame the mind
and quell the uproar of negative emotions.* Judy Lief

MAKING PEOPLE WAIT in my courtroom because I'm late is my favorite power play but today I relish every moment. Right now there are three of them, his father standing beside him, to his left, and the venerable Magallan Rinboku, on his right, Mahá stands waiting, practicing mindful patience. I'm sure they think my being twenty minutes late is a sign of my incompetence. Today, in this meeting, I will assign Mahá a position in my Royal court.

There are two open positions in the court. One is for the Ambassador of Commerce, and if Mahá is offered this position, he would work with his father, the Royal Treasurer. The other opportunity is the Ambassador of the King's Guard, meaning Mahá would spend his days traveling alone across the planet. However, there is a third position. It is a Royal position that none of them expected since his father was certain he had persuaded me not to assign it to his boy.

I enter my court and walk past the three men. The sound of my little feet walking across the rock-tiled floor causing a faint echo off the walls. The echoes sound like a person tapping their fingertips on a tabletop.

I ask, "How has married life found you, Mahá? What is it, one year since the wedding?"

Mahá answers, "Yes. In three days it will be a year. I find it satisfying."

I take a seat in my grand chair. I say, "We've never spoken before, and I presume you're feeling timid. What with speaking with me, the King of our world. So I want to give you a chance. That is, I'll make this a one-time exception. However, I expect you to speak loud and confident when addressing me. I scorn quiet and disregard timid people."

Mahá didn't flinch or change his expression when he responds with a voice of confidence and clarity. "I'm certain that you never spoke with me. You seldom speak to anyone in our world. So perhaps my voice was quiet when I answered because I have been standing here in silence for over twenty minutes waiting for you to arrive. But I am not timid."

Mahá's father is distressed as he speaks. "Mahá, speak to our King with respect."

"Hold that," I interrupt. "Let the boy speak. The days of needing his father to guide him have passed. He's offended that I ignore showing reverence to him and the venerable Rinboku. I haven't invited any of you to sit with me at my table either. And he believes I'm late. But, as the King of our planet, I will tell you this, Mahá I hold the privilege for these and more."

Mahá's father nodded at me in agreement. The two of us spoke for several hours yesterday about this meeting. I was not willing to put Mahá in the position of Ambassador of Commerce but at the end of the conversation, I agreed that I would.

Following yesterday's meeting and unknown to the King, Mahá's father met with his son and told him he had nothing to worry about tomorrow's meeting. "I promise you the King

will make you Ambassador of Commerce and the two of us will
work on many projects together," he told his son.

Sitting back in my big chair I analyze the boy's answer. Everyone told me that Mahá is charismatic and that he is confident. I'll agree. He's likable, good-looking, and he's big too. I think he's the biggest man I ever saw. There's something about him. I get a sense he is special and holds the essence of leadership. I don't like that. Not one bit!

Dramatic and beautiful, my courtroom is comparable to a museum where the walls display many of my paintings and large shelves are decorated with my sculptures. There's a long table with chairs on each side to accommodate twelve, with my raised chair at the head.

Most of my art illustrates the bio-molecularity of plants—grains and legumes. My ancestors are a lineage of bio-molecular scientists.

My skills in painting and sculpting are exceptional. Many of those privileged to see my courtroom say the art is a display of perfection. There are ornate pots filled with beautiful plants and cut flowers. Plants and flowers are my passion, and I insist on perfection in each display.

The Humanoids built the palace, and all the city's architecture was done by them long before the first people arrived. As a result, the architecture is ornate and elegant. And while color is absent, there is also a notable departure from fascism, as found in government and royalty buildings on other human-settled planets.

@@@@@

"Mahá, your father is the best friend I've ever known, and he's also my most valuable member of the Royal Council. You must uphold tradition and follow his lead." My right hand fondles the large, square, gawu box amulet dangling around my neck. "So answer me this, Mahá as the second clan of the forty-four, what is your family vow of duty?"

In the Buddha's instructions on Earth, he produced forty-four
laws for assuring social harmony. The Humanoids assigned
each of the ancestral families one of the forty-four laws. Each

lineage is committed to being the pillar of that assigned law for the people.

Mahá responds to my question fast, loud, and precise, "My family upholds the second law, which states, 'Others will destroy life; we shall abstain from the destruction of life here.'"

I pound my fist on the arm of the chair and the faint sound echoes off the walls and ceiling of the courtroom. "Well said, and my family upholds the first law, which states, 'Others will inflict harm; we shall not inflict harm here.' I felt you harmed me when the Oracle spoke at your wedding ceremony. It was the most unpleasant experience. The Oracle announced to the entire universe that you, Mahá would become King of the planet. After the Oracle spoke those words (an epiphany of the future), I was harmed."

Mahá thinks back to the wedding ceremony a year ago at the outdoor amphitheater. At the time of the Oracle giving the prediction for him and his wife, Visákhá. He recalls the memory . . .

At the end of the third rotation around them, the Oracle stops in front of Mahá. The Oracle looks into Mahá's eyes. Then, as fast as a lump of hot coal burns your fingertips when plucked out of the fire, the Oracle grabs Mahá's head with both hands. Mahá startled by the movement, resists and struggles to free himself from the grasp. The Oracle's grip is firm, and as Mahá struggles, he soon realizes he cannot break free from the unimaginable strength of the Oracle. Mahá surrenders, relaxes his posture, and calms his mind.

The Oracle forces their foreheads together, and they stand right there, head to head for several seconds. Everyone present notices a slight twitch from the Oracle's body. It was a very slight twitch, but just as you would think maybe you hadn't seen it, there was another. Now it is obvious—there is movement—as the Oracle begins to stamp, and the whole body begins to shake and vibrate out of control. When at long last, the Oracle released his hold on Mahá swung his hands straight out to the side with a burst of energy that sent Mahá falling backward and onto the ground. Mahá jumped up onto his feet and moved back to where the Oracle had placed him. The Oracle stands with arms outstretched and face turned up and speaks aloud the fortune, the prediction for Mahá's future.

Oracle says, "There is a path with two directions. In one direction, Mahá works every day in the King's court. Before the end of two years, he will rule the kingdom. In the other direction, Mahá works as the King's Guardian. Before the end of four years, he will rule the Galaxy and all humans."

When the King starts to speak again, Mahá ends his thoughts of the wedding and listens.

"Some people think I rule with the temperament of a child. They say I'm stubborn and demanding, too. What do you say, Mahá Do you think I'm childish and challenging?"

The venerable Magallan Rinboku clears his throat in preparation to speak. Indeed, my tough questioning seems unnecessary to Magallan. He and I had a meeting last week and Like Mahá's father, Magallan wanted me not to put the boy in charge of my gardens. The Abbot of the monastery, Magallan, came to know how powerful Mahá's cognitive mind is. He feels the boy would do the community the most benefit by working in the commerce position. I agreed not to place Mahá in charge of the gardens. But before Magallan could say a word, Mahá spoke.

"The King is a perfectionist, not a child. It is Kung Fu," Mahá says. "Our existence requires mastery of our actions. The perfection of thoughts must be in harmony with the perfection of the body. This is called Kung Fu. I find you to be a King who mastered Kung Fu."

"Kung Fu is indeed correct, " I reply. "You are the sole person to realize the purpose of my fascination with perfection. I spoke with your father at length regarding your position. Likewise, I spoke to Rinboku about granting you a position as well. Your father disagrees with my first choice for you, and Rinboku told me you, Mahá have great power."

@@@@@

The King's tiny face and features remind Mahá of a recurring dream. When he looks at the King's small frame seated on his large throne, he seems like a child all dressed up playing king for a day.

Mahá slips into a daydream recalling the dreamscape:—*I'm talking with a man who is also of small stature but he's not the King. Whereas the King's voice is high-pitched and his words are over-emphasized, exaggerated with adverbs, and when he talks he sings but he is out of tune.*

The man from the dream is soft-spoken, and he is also well-spoken and he's trying to explain something of importance, though I cannot understand why, or what is so significant. He's a holy man from a distant planet (maybe Earth). I ask him why it is impossible for us to transcend? What is holding people here in this present moment and how does life make it impossible for us to choose to come and go as we wish?

"Mara sprung the trap," he answered. "We are bound in the existence of her making. Mara invented this duality. It was on the day when she stepped through a black hole from a different universe. Her body and essence were ripped apart by the black hole even to the molecular level and smaller. For billions of years now the event has been known as the Big Bang and the creation of our known universe.

"Many philosophies and theories suggest that this universe, we call Samsara, will end when Mara recognizes herself in all the creations. Everything that exists in this universe is made from Mara. Some think it will be in human form that she will awaken and remember. At that instant, everything will cease to exist. Until then, we are trapped in this dream-like state of being."

After his explanation, and after taking several minutes to myself evaluating how the words affect me, I said, "Mara, in an act of suicide, destroyed herself. Everything on this side of that black hole is the result of her death and everything is limited by death. Everything that has a beginning will end. Planets, stars, people, with one exception: Energy.

The essence of her life never goes away; it is always in motion and forever changing. Did I get that right?" I ask the holy man.

At this point in my recurring dream, the holy man is sitting in a floating chair that is made of multi-colored lights beaming in all directions. The lights change in color and pulse, twinkle and stream.

"Consciousness is the common thread. There is the potential for consciousness in everything, but the illusions of self distract us from awakening. The meaning of life isn't to live a life. It is instead to awaken to the consciousness of the True Self.

"Imagine the great wealth and benefit the True-Self awakens to. When your ego-self stops doing for the ego, awakens to consciousness then you begin to love everything and everybody as if it is all one True-Self." He laughed in delight and said, "Try to help everybody in every moment of the heart beating in the form called, me. The I dissolves into a perception of we. Then after practicing charitable life, soon 'we' dissolves and there just is. What you might call, isness." He laughs with delight and a smile bright as the lights that beam from his floating chair fill my eyes.

"One last word to be aware of before I leave. Karma is the result of action. It is both the cause and the effect. For every action (doing) there is an effect (result). The merit of actions that benefit the True Self is returned in the heaven realms. The merit of all other actions is delivered in the hell realms, animal realms, and the human realm. As if by magic it is only in the human realm that we get the possibility of awakening to actions that bring great wealth and opportunity. Always silence the ego-self. Silence the thinking mind. Awake the True Self. Return to The Source.

"Samsara is the cycle of karma. Birth leads to aging, sickness, and death. Over and over again the cycle continues. Your rebirth may be in the heaven realm but even there, life is temporary. You may be reborn in one of the hell realms, but even in hell life is temporary. In every birth your karma is used up through that lifetime, it is the energy that you made previously. Once you burn off the karma in one realm, you die. Maybe

you will be reborn again before Mara wakes. Maybe you won't. Life is a miracle."

"What happens if Mara recognizes herself in this existence and wakes up before we can liberate our True-Self?" I ask.

"One thing is for certain regarding her waking. She has not yet woken."

"How do you know?" I ask.

"Because we are having this conversation." He laughed with great delight and he floats away.

I'm watching the holy man floating away in his chair made of light. But now I hear the King's high-pitched voice saying something to me about power. I stop daydreaming and focus on the present moment back here in the King's court standing with my father, and the venerable Magallan. The King is speaking.

@@@@@

"Power is a subject I can relate to. Power is an addiction. At least it can be when paired with privilege. Therefore, I bear reservations as the Oracle revealed you would become King if I gave you a job within my court." My fists pound against the arms of my high throne. *This boy wants to take my place as King. He's strong-willed, intelligent, and his confidence threatens me. I've learned plenty about this Mahá today that I didn't know before.*

"However, based on what I learned about you today, Mahá I appoint you to the position of Ambassador of the Palace Garden. From today and always."

Mahá's father and Magallan moan and grumble. Magallan rings the prayer bell he holds in his left hand and turns the dorje in his right. Unmoved by their audible and visible protests, I continue with my appointing for the position.

"I had many Royal families detached from the Royal council because they failed in this position. Therefore, placing you as Ambassador of the Garden causes me a great deal of discomfort. Almost as much pain as the Oracle caused me at your wedding." I leap down out of my throne, the chair squeals as it slides across the stone floor, and then I slap my bare hand on top of the long table. My eyes locked with Mahá.

"Do you understand, Mahá? If you fail in this position, your household will no longer be a Royal family, and do you know all the repercussions of being removed from Royalty?"

The second rainstorm is gathering full strength outside, and a gust of wind forces the chamber door open. The door slams against the wall with a crash and leaves, dust, and farm plant debris come flying in with the gust. Mahá always sturdy as a stone pillar, walks over to close the door. A loud clap of thunder gets muffled as he pushes the door firm against the jam.

Mahá's father stood fast, I can imagine his mind filled with conflicting thoughts and fears. Fears of his son being given the worst position on my council. Also, the fear of his entire lineage being expelled from Royal status and removed from the mountaintop city. His conflict with our entrusted friendship and me having promised him yesterday that I wouldn't assign the Ambassador of Garden to his son.

His father and I have been friends since we were children. Our relationship grew over the years, and we are best friends. Our friendship made him feel confident that his son would thrive in any position but this one. For my peace of mind, I gave the boy this position. If Mahá tries to take my place as King, I will squash his entire family long before he can take the first step.

The boy answers me with determination, "Yes. I understand the requirements and the consequences."

"This meeting is finished," I said. That was it. The end of our meeting. I stepped around the table where I stood in front of them long enough to meet eye-to-eye with each one. These three must think I'm a fool. Their plot to sneak this boy into my court and ease me off the throne is obvious to me. While they look up to see if I'm throwing a snare over their heads, they're unaware. The whole time they run their game, my foot, below their view, rests on top of the lever that opens the trapdoor below their feet. Not a word as I stomped across the floor.

Mahá can sense from the King's words as well as the fear in his voice that the King is full of pride, conceit, and fear of losing his power. The King strips away other people's titles and homes, acting out his own fears of having the same done to him. But, Mahá too is filled with self-doubt and fear. All of his friends and the monks at the monastery tell him he will be the King one day. That they believe in his strength of mind as The First Priority. But Mahá doesn't share their confidence.

@@@@@@

After the King was out of the courtroom. Magallan and Mahá's father were expressing their disappointment in the meeting's result. Mahá says, "Please stop worrying about the assignment and my ability to serve the King."

Magallan smiled and agreed. "You possess the gift of leadership and the divine help of the Bodhisattvas. I should try to exercise more faith."

Mahá leads the three of them out of the courtroom and down the path toward Main Road. "Faith is nothing more than a word describing a mental escape from life. None of us should hold on to faith. Knowledge and wisdom are what we seek."

Then Magallan and Mahá's father got in the cart to leave the palace, but Mahá stayed behind. "Aren't you coming with us to the monastery?" Mahá shook his head, then waved them farewell. After they were out of sight, Mahá went to meet with Merliana. She's the Chief Judge of the King's Court. She was waiting for him as he made the appointment several days before.

Merliana greets him as he enters her courtroom. "Hello, Mahá Rinboku. How can I help you? I've been eager for our meeting since you made the appointment and excited to see how I can assist."

"You are so kind, Merliana," he says. "There are three subjects of concern, and I want to address them with care and respect. My concerns are genuine, but my concerns are confrontational too. First, I want to reinstate all the people who have been told they are no longer a Royal Family. There is nothing in our doctrine of community which provides anyone, even the King, with the power to change who is a Royal Family."

Merliana asks him to continue, "The second of the three concerns. Please continue."

"Three families were told to move out of their homes and to leave the top of the mountain to take up residence in the orchards village below. They were told that since they are no longer Royal, they must do this. My second concern is that there are no homes below for these families. They had to find other families to share a residence with and there are no resources for the children to attend school either. Each day, their children take a cart to the top of the mountain to attend school, and the parents have to do the same. They take a cart to get to their fields and work. Twice a day each to get to school and work and then to return to the orchards village to the shared homes.

"Carts are being used for transportation when they should be for farming and producing crops. People's motivations are being distracted as well as crops being lost. Yesterday I told those three families to go back to their homes on top of the mountain. The third subject is the King's dementia. It is becoming more of a detriment to the community with each passing day. This entire initiative for the use of privilege to the Royals is a disease and a poison. It causes suffering to non-Royal families as it made them feel inferior and suffering to Royal families when used as leverage enforcing certain performance behavior."

Merliana says nothing, as she weighs all he has said. Her posture as she sits behind her large ornate desk is straight, and you can't even see her moving to breathe. She's in her early thirties and a mother of three children. She's average height, and her figure shows her age and its effects after bearing three children. Shoulder-length yellow hair, with bright green eyes. People feel accepted and appreciated when in her presence and her tone further puts them at ease.

"It is a problem that isn't easy to help you with, nor is it pleasing to hear. You don't have the authority to overturn the King's directions. What consequence of your actions? Might I ask you who you have in mind to ascend to the throne if we judges decide we must replace him?"

"That's not for me to say or to choose," Mahá was quick to reply.

"Yet you feel it is within your authority to countermand the King and to request he abdicates his place in our community? Don't answer that. You've already said more than you should. While I will not decide today, I will discuss your three concerns with the other judges. Is there anything more, Mahá?"

"Nothing more, Merliana. Other than to thank you for meeting with me and allowing me to express these concerns."

Merliana still hasn't moved. Mahá wondered if she had even blinked or taken a breath the whole meeting. Even as she speaks, she is absent of expression physically and in tone. Her eyes never look away from the person she talks with. Though she has been Chief Judge for less than two years, she has perfected the personification of a Royal Judge.

"I wish you all the best in your new position on the King's court. Goodbye for now," she says.

@@@@@@

Following the King's court appointment, and his meeting with Merliana, Mahá's days became routine. First, he wakes to a modest breakfast with the love of his life, Visákhá. The first meal is always shared with the sharecroppers, cooks, and housekeepers at the long table in the kitchen. The smell of fresh-baked bread, pies, and soups fills the house as does the conversations between the hungry group. Then he's off to the growers to pick up the King's fresh-cut flowers.

He meets with the landscapers and the palace maintenance crew at the center of town to go over their progress and needs for the day.

Then he takes the fresh-cut flowers to the King's courtyard, halls, and courtroom to decorate and arrange the decor. Finally, he waits for the King to enter the courtroom. Then after a brief conversation, Mahá leaves the palace and goes to the Monastery to teach the law, meditate, and exercise his body and mind.

At long last, he goes home to relax on his deck in his favorite Adirondack chair. There he combs his fingers through his thick soft beard while counting the clouds in the sky, watches the wind pass over the valley below as it whips through the orchards and nut trees. And he waits for his lover to join him. Together they watch the binary stars and clouds crossing the sky, and they talk about their day's activities until it's time for sleep.

Twice a week, the routine includes Vallena. She's Visákhá's BFF and comes up to the top of the mountain on the third day of the week. She stays with Mahá and Visákhá for two days. Kelv, Mahá's BFF, comes to their house on both of those days to visit. Kelv and Vallena develop a magical rapport, and he holds Vallena's heart.

Kelv committed to the path of a Bodhisattva, but Vallena pledged to give her love to him even though she knows he'll never take a wife, and he lives a celibate life. Vallena and Kelv spend the latter part of the day walking through the crowded fields of Mahá's farm as they discuss her work and his quest. Often they'll stay up talking until the start of the next day.

Visákhá manages the farm, and, as she promised, she committed all the land and the sharecroppers to grow Vallena's cannabis plants. The plants provide fibers to produce ultraviolet and X-ray protective fabrics and are key ingredients for pharmaceuticals.

Vallena's days are spent working on new plant strains, while Visákhá focuses on higher production, new fiber uses, and drug applications. The challenges of living on a planet with a binary star are many, but the extraordinary benefits from Vallena's and Visákhá's efforts are nothing short of miraculous.

It is anger, the Buddha said, that is the single human emotion that can instantly erase, destroy, and undo all merit. Anger is the enemy of those who desire liberation from Samsara. Through a million actions of earning merit of great wealth and opportunity by helping others, a single instance of anger will destroy all that merit. When the Humanoids discovered the serum that removes anger from the DNA, they theorized humanity's destiny was written.

The people on Planet 444 are all born free of anger. They wear thick full-body robes that are designed to protect them from the x-rays that are emitted from one of the stars their plant revolves around. They wear hoods and eye protection as well. But as the smaller star's gravity tugs on the x-ray-emitting neutron star, it changes its wobble and causes more intense emissions. Sharecroppers grow marijuana plants to use the flowers in producing pharmaceuticals that help fight radiation poisoning. The fibers from the plants are used to make more protective clothing as well as glass coating for the windows of their homes.

The routines are clockwork, and friendships continue to flourish. But life here is the same as it is everywhere; the one certainty in life is change. The question is, is it changing for the good?

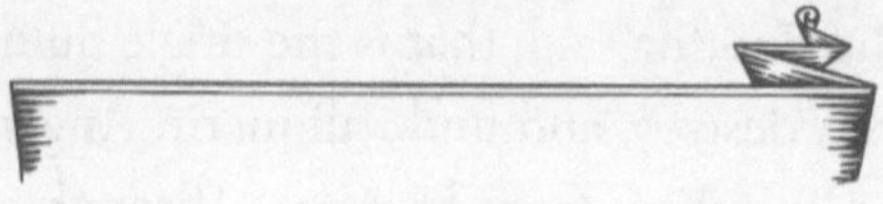

Chapter 2 -> Words Have Power

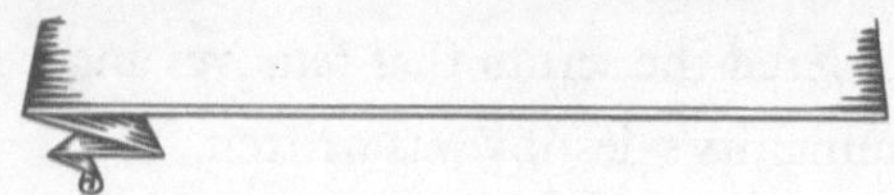

<u>**Sara**</u>
Drowning
in the sea of love
*where everyone would love to drown*Stevie Nicks

VISÁKHÁ (WIFE TO MAHÁ) tells this story on the day of their second wedding anniversary. One year after the King gave Mahá the position in the King's court as Ambassador of Gardens.

Startled for a moment as I slid my slender and short body into the Adirondack chair next to him. Oops, maybe not so slender as my wide hips and round butt bounce when I hit the seat of the chair. The near-perfect chair maneuver manages to distract Mahá from his favorite amusement of watching the valley below.

The front porch of our home is twenty meters away from a thousand meters high sheer cliff at the edge of the mountain top. My husband (Mahá) often loses hours a day sitting and watching the beauty of the hill shadows, and cloud shadows as they dance across the valley floor. He can see the orchards and the giant nut tree groves as the wind moves their heavy branches covered in dense leaves and abundant fruits.

"I see you're busy counting clouds and chasing shadows again." I tease him while I hand him a large glass of his favorite beverage.

He's careful not to show it, but I can tell he worries. There's so much on his plate with the meeting between him and the King and the appointment to the King's court. According to the Oracle, on our wedding day. Mahá will soon become King and I'll die before our children's seventh year. Preposterous, I say, but it still shakes me to my core. He also worries because we all know he is bound to accomplish the First Priority once he is King. He hasn't accepted himself to be the great being that he is.

Our ancestors foretold the next King, our generation, to be the King who fulfills the promise of Nirvaning. These sorts of proverbs never materialize in the way we expect. This proverb foretells when our grand experiment, or what we like to call ourselves—the community—discovers Nirvana. Mahá suspects the DNA-altering serum isn't the needed ingredient. "Being free of anger doesn't provide consciousness with the emptiness that is necessary for the first priority (being Nirvanad)," he reminds me of this every day.

Anyway, all that aside, today is our second anniversary. He shares a smile of appreciation and boin, accepting the glass from my hands. "I have been wanting to ask you a question all day," He says.

"Ask me." Before he could blink, I responded.

"It's an anniversary question." He sets his glass down on the porch next to his chair. He points a finger at me and then points the finger at himself in rapid repetition as he asks. "What is this thing we share? If you say it is love, you are wrong, and if you say it is anything else, you are wrong. What is this?" He settles back into his chair, waiting for my response.

Mahá knows the question is a novice Koan and simplistic for someone as advanced in mindfulness as I am. The more profound lesson of the Koan was learned long ago. But he's intrigued to watch how I'll respond to this romantic twist.

Out of the corner of his eye, he sees me put my glass down and stand up from my chair. With the humility of a sex slave, I drop my dark coffee-colored body onto my hands and knees. Slow and seductive, I crawl over to him and onto his lap. He takes me in his caramel-colored arms and I curl my legs and torso upon his upper body. Laying my head on his shoulder, I bury my face into his neck; kissing and nibbling at the flesh there.

"Yes. I agree." He says. "This is what it is." The glow of love on his face and the twinkle of desire in his eyes.

Vallena and Kelv are standing in the shadows, close enough to see Mahá and me and hear what we said. I know she's there. I've always been able to sense her presence. So we share a mysterious but unmistakable centimetric detection of one another's presence.

I can hear Vallena whispering to Kelv, not interrupting the moment. "Passionate love like theirs is like a rich, spicy broth. Assembled to extract flavor from an abundance of ingredients and blend them as the broth gets cooked down, add in more broth and cook it down, again and again, condensing into an experience of deep intensity. Each sip of the broth makes the lovers crave another sip, and then another and another until they become intoxicated and addicted. But take care, any small deviation, even the slightest ripple in the relationship, leads to intense personal suffering and will lead the couple down in a negative spiral."

Kelv and Vallena step out of the shadows and walk up the steps to join Mahá and me on the porch. "Look at this pair," Kelv says with his hands pressed together in front of him as he bows to us. "Two years of marriage and they're still in honeymoon mode."

Vallena quips, "I could drink them up like a cool glass of water on a hot day."

I greet them without budging from my husband's embrace, "Hi my friends. Boin you're joining us on our anniversary day." Of all our closest friends, Mahá and I always felt it would be the four of us (Vallena, Kelv, Mahá, and me) who would change the course of our society. Everyone in the group is required, but the grist would depend on our strengths.

@@@@@

Soon, we are joined by many friends, and the celebration begins with a feast. Midway through the meal of well-sauced and seasoned beans, legumes, and crisp vegetables, a popular band arrives to perform my favorite, tribal music, for the party. The guests are Airodia and his wife, Utotutua. Airodia is a leading physicist for the community and Utotutua is a medical doctor and recently certified as a surgeon. Merliana, a member of the King's court as Chief Royal Judge, also manages the Village City Council. Shavarah and Kyphi are also representatives of the King's court and manage the city council and commerce for the upper city. And then there's Drrea and Danip, who are both research scientists. Drrea is leading the manufacturing of fabrics and making clothing from cannabis plant fibers. Danip develops revolutionary methods for land management, which extract the most for plants while preserving the farm and orchard lands for the long term.

Upon entering our house from the large wrap-around porch you pass through the double doors and into an open-concept living room, dining, and kitchen. Our home is well-equipped with large rectangular pillows, drum pillows, and sitting pillows for meditation. There are a few lounge chairs, but Mahá and I prefer pillows. A long table runs along the kitchen island where the sharecroppers and house staff gather for daily meals. Otherwise, the floor is wide open to throw a pillow down and take a seat or lounge across a few pillows to relax.

The huge front-facing window is coated with a radiation-filtering glaze and allows the natural light to fill the house safely. In the distance, the view opens up to the ocean that covers most of our planet. The yellow sky and ever-changing pink and orange cloud formations captivate everyone's attention. Two violent storms roll in daily, covering the valley below us with clouds. The band will always set up here in front of the window during parties using the ever-changing sky as their backdrop.

Planet 444 is illuminated by a binary star system consisting of a neutron star and a white dwarf. The X-ray emission from the neutron star we call, Kelly, forces us to wear full-length protective robes for most of the day. When Kelly is twenty degrees above the horizon, we also need to wear hoods and eye protection. Most of us use this time of day for sleeping and otherwise stay indoors. It takes seven hours for Kelly to cycle above and below the danger zone. The dwarf star, we call Faust (for the famous alchemist Edward Kelly, who later made the legend of Faust House famous), seldom drifts below the horizon. Once every four years, there is a fourteen-day period when it slips out of sight.

"I've been curious about our ancestors," Airodia told the group as the band took a break, "I'm wondering why the Humanoids decided that the first twelve families are Royal while the remaining thirty-two families make up the common population. It is a caste society where Royal families marry other Royals, and common marry common families. Then, of course, Royals work for the King's court, and common families work the fields, orchards, and commerce."

Danip replies with a leading question, "Yes, a caste society, but also a monarchy. We've known one another since we were children, but I don't know your household numbers. How did the Humanoids decide which family was number one and so on down to the forty-fourth?"

Mahá was the first to answer, "My lineage is number two, we shall not destroy life here, is our banner. The intention for the clan numbers is to help us live by the laws Shakyamuni Buddha provides." He performs the Vitarka Mudra while continuing to speak.

"The laws for communal living written in the Vinaya are forty-four in number with the first twelve being more Monastic, and the remaining are more for laypeople. But aside from our knowledge of it, not one of our Royals lives up to the intention."

For people who are not free from anger, there would be at least one person showing outrage at the lack of leadership for enforcing the laws. Likewise, and by contrast, the community on Planet 444 is free from anger, and therefore they say and listen to everything with peaceful and accepting enthusiasm rather than anger.

Airodia spoke next as the group continued to go around the room in clockwise rotation, sharing family numbers and lineage oath, "My family is number seven; we abstain from false speech here."

Utotutua says, "My family is assigned number ten and our oath is, bless all beings to be free of suffering and the causes of suffering." Shavarah spoke next. "Mine is family three. We hold the responsibility for the oath; we abstain from taking what is not given here." Merliana says, "My heritage vowed to keep everyone working together and living together as a whole. The actual words from Shakyamuni are hard to grasp when you first hear them (Abstain from divisive speech.). But we want to use words that pull us together as one people united in our efforts. That's family number six," Merliana shrugs playfully and laughs.

Kyphi is next, and she says, "Mine is family eleven and we are responsible for the oath; we are of right view here."

Drrea, always demonstrative, leaps to his feet and stands tall, well, tall for him. He's just a few inches taller than I am. Pretentious, he bows before telling the group, "I come from family thirty-five, and we are the oath keepers of, we shall have good friends here." Danip pulls on Drrea's arm to get him to sit back down as he tells the group of friends, "My family is number nineteen, and our banner is, we shall be of right knowledge here."

Kelv looks at everybody around the room and says, "The oaths and banners are insignificant under this monarchy. Even our so-called family numbers are unimportant in our pathless community today. But to keep the party going, I'll play along. My family was the last chosen to be Royal. Whatever that is thought to mean. I'm from family number twelve, and our oath slash banner is, we shall be of right intention here."

Under normal circumstances, where people don't have anger removed from their DNA, Kelv's anti-government words could spark an angry confrontation among the group. Even his tone would be fiery and it would ignite confrontation. But, wholehearted, this community finds pleasure in everyone's words and ideas.

Vallena is still laughing as she blows a kiss across the room toward Kelv. "What would a party be like without a philosophical speech from our brother Kelv? He pretends to catch her blown kiss and then he stuffs it inside the gawu box of his necklace. "Chibusa!" She laughs and then says, "Mine is family number forty and we are the oath keepers for, we shall be of great learning here."

I waited until everyone else finished. Then, pressing the palms of my hands together held at the heart chakra with thumbs resting lightly against my sternum, I perform the Namaskara Mudra. "I come from family number one. My ancestral grandfather was a physics scientist specializing in developing a theory for electromagnetism's effect on the organic human mind. So the Humanoids chose him first for his achievements in science. Well, anyway, our lineage is responsible for the oath; we shall not inflict harm here."

@@@@@

Airodia says, "Boin, everyone. So, now my curiosity is met with confusion. Let me try to explain. Well, let's see. Where to start? Okay, other than marriage and appointments to positions in the King's court, our population all live, work, shop, eat and play without segregation. We all share the same medical care, quality of homes, education, shopping, and common areas in our community. Nothing in society provides better living conditions for some and lesser for others. We are living in equanimity, united and happy."

"I disagree." The words are out of my mouth before I can stop myself. "Except that Royals do enjoy privileges. Royals are given access to comps and use it to gain access to restricted areas, and they use their family number to take more in commerce too."

Airodia is surprised and asks, "What do you mean that Royals take more?"

I turn to look at Drrea and ask him, "The new robes you're making with the UV and radiation protective fibers. How many robes did you take for yourself?"

Drrea answers, "I have three. But they protect from X-ray, not radiation."

"And you Vallena? You made it possible for all people to own these new fibers. How many robes do you have?"

Vallena was hesitant to respond, but the room stayed quiet, waiting for her to respond. At long last, she answers, "I took two."

Then I turn to face Shavarah, from a Royal family, asking her. "Your family number three, and yourself a member of the King's court, Shavarah. How many new robes did you take?" She responds, "I think it's fourteen. But there are so many new colors now. Before there was bone white and nothing else. I want to own two of each of the new colors. It's important in my Royal position to represent the new technology to the community. With these new robes, we can see each other. You know, the thick fabric of the old robes hid our features and protected us from the binary stars' radiation. They were total burkas, but the new fibers are near transparent. Some of them are very transparent."

Merliana was deep in thought and hardly noticed when Kyphi clipped one of the pillows out from under her. As the chief judge of the Royal Council, she hadn't realized the divisive nature of the King's Royal Privileges. The privilege of a few will not promote the First Priority. Her face showed confusion and concern following this conversation among her friends.

The band was back from their break, bringing with them the distinct smells of fresh ganja smoke. As they begin to play, Mahá stands and performs the Vitarka Mudra and says, "Wait! Before we get running full speed down this rabbit hole of diverse privilege, I want to say two things. First, I want to ask Vallena to share some of her new ganja weed. She tells me it delivers a magical quality fit for our creative needs."

Before he finished the sentence, Vallena had already pulled her fogger from her backpack and passed it around. Mahá continues, "Second, Visákhá made her point that the Royal families are becoming greedy.

"However, I want to point out this is an example of how words carry power. So, let me say because all of us have forgotten these forty-four laws were established to guide us. Our civilization neglects the intention of the forty-four declarations. The Buddha's forty-four laws guide humankind to accomplish The First Priority. Following the law provides great wealth and opportunity for the individual and society. Therefore, pointing blame and shining a light on misguided leadership should instead be for us, and I mean those of us in this room, for all of us, my friends, an opportunity to remind the community of our First Priority."

@@@@@

With that said, I say, "Drrea and Vallena, are you ready to heat this party up, ladies?" The three of us jump to our feet and gather together in front of the band. We are standing side by side, facing our friends. We take off our robes and toss them aside. Beneath them, we are wearing outfits similar to 23rd century Earth, belly dancing made from the new fabric. The garments are sensual, silky, and see-through, depending on the visual angle and light.

Drrea is a beautiful man with a short, muscular, stocky body and an absolute knockout punch beautiful man-package. The skin tone of his scrotum and shaft is like buttercream frosting, and while he isn't hung like a Hollywood porn star, he's perfect. Even straight men can't ignore the beauty of his junk. His face is gorgeous though if you look close, his left eye is larger than the right, and his nose is bent to the left. His inviting thick lips beg attention and I have taken up kissing him when we greet and again when we say goodbye because those lips are delicious—so kissable.

Vallena was born with a skin pigmentation condition (vitiligo), and at first glance, you would think she is a burn victim. Her tom-boy personality fits her very tall and very boyish body. She has no hips, no butt, and her breasts are small, with the nipples and areolas are too large. Her hair is shiny and as black as space. Her voice is bold and smooth and she speaks so slow; at times, it almost hurts to listen to her. Her hazel-brown eyes can hypnotize, and a soft, long face with a shallow chin and high cheeks.

As for me, well, I already said I'm short and slender with wide hips and a mighty round ass. My hair is super short, black with tight curls, and my breasts aren't huge but not small. There's for sure more than a handful. I remember Drrea and Vallena agreed, several days ago when we were rehearsing our dance, that my titties are very pinchable. My eyes are dark and slanted upward a bit on the corners. The bridge of my nose is too wide, and the end is too round. It's my worst feature. My lips are full but not puffy, and my chin rounds out my face. I don't go anywhere without my round, gawu box, necklace.

We perform a well-rehearsed ritual dance. The band cranks up the sound as our dance starts with several hoots and whistles from the party. Before we ditched our robes, Kelv slips out of the house unnoticed by everyone except, myself and of course, Vallena. She knew that he wouldn't be able to watch her and the three of us perform the seductive dances. Kelv is our new spiritual leader. I'm convinced he will be critical to The First Priority.

@@@@@

Everyone continues to smoke the ganja, and soon they are dancing and grinding to the beat. I managed to snap Merliana out of her funk and she dances with me and Airodia. There's something about dancing and letting loose to music that moves without words that can heal your heart. It's time spent where the mind and the body are in sync, where the only objective is to be.

Finally, after several hours of performing, the band announces they are finishing up after one more song. As soon as they call the last song, Vallena makes her way over to where Mahá is sitting. He's taking a break from the dance and sitting on the floor on top of a barrel pillow with his back against the wall.

I watch as she seats her very tall, leggy, and boyish-shaped body in a lotus position on the floor straight across, less than ten centimeters between their knees, in front of him. Her naked and very female body was exposed through transparent garments. High on the ganja and unashamed, she asks him, "Can you come with me tomorrow? I want to show you something that is growing in my garden. Kelv said he will cover your class tomorrow at the monastery. I've got something that you can use to blow the King's mind. So please, please, please, will you come down the mountain with me?"

Vallena and I can sense each other's presence, but I also know her well enough; she knows what she's doing. Teasing the men and getting a rise out of them make her feel attractive and powerful. But I told her time and time again her teasing will result in a bad consequence sooner or later.

Mahá is also well-baked and tries not to be distracted by Vallena's stark naked and pigment-deformed, odd-looking skin. He half chokes as he replies, "Yes." Then he clears his throat and tries to maintain eye to eye with her. He says, "Yes. Of course. I, I—well, I look forward to seeing everything you have. I mean, to see what you're going to show me." He stumbles to his feet, embarrassed at his words and not knowing how to recover with any grace. He tells her as he walks out the door to join Kelv on the porch. "I'll pick you up in my cart after I finish at the palace tomorrow."

The band finished playing soon after that, and everyone went home. Mahá, Kelv, and Drrea stayed out on the porch talking while Vallena and I went off to bed.

"There's only another hour and a half before Kelly hits the danger zone," Kelv says as the two men join him on the wrap-around deck outside. "The band better hustle if they are going to get their equipment packed and get home on time."

"There's something on my mind that I want to share with you guys, "Mahá says. I can hear the three of them talking as I lay in bed trying to relax enough to fall asleep. Mahá says, "Something must have been pretty horrible for Mara to jump into a black hole to kill herself. There must be unimaginable grief to get to a point in your life where killing yourself is easier than fighting on. This makes me wonder then as all of us on this planet fight onward for the First Priority (liberation) are we liberating our True-Self, or are we liberating Mara's True-Self? I'm sensing that these are the same thing. Nirvanaing is an all-encompassing transcendence."

Super amazing awareness Mahá" says Drrea. "There are so many gaps in the teaching on everything from the Buddha and the Arhats. All of the content we learn from and study is based on Earthlings, and living on Earth. Most of the metaphors and similes don't make any sense for people living on other planets. Which I think is why we run into these sorts of mental traps."

"You're onto something with this thought, Drrea," Mahá says. "Earth religions are not universal? This may be true in many ways, besides the information having been written by people on Earth. Perhaps every civilized planet will evolve, invent and discover its gods. Perhaps the difficulty isn't that we can't transcend, it's that we can't succeed following Earth's gods and philosophies on Planet Four Four Four."

"We need to go now or we will spend the sleep hours here," says Kelv.

"What are your thoughts on this, Kelv?" asks Drrea.

"I'm certain there is something easier than what we strain our brains to comprehend," Kelv explains. " In this purgatory, as Mahá bracketed our universe, we are trying to transcend through intellect instead of through—isness. Look at Kelly out there in the universe. It doesn't know it's a neutron star. It doesn't know it emits X-rays with every quake. It just is. It neither tries nor contemplates itself. It just is.

"There is a proverb from the Dao that says, one should aim to be useless. The example explains a forest on the edge of a large community of people. All of the useful trees have been cut down and used to make planks for people's homes. The only trees left to thrive and live in peace are the useless trees. The crooked, bent, and odd-shaped trees don't know they are useless. They just live."

Drrea says, "Chibusa. That is my new favorite lesson and it also is an example of what I said. What is a forest? And all of the trees here are fruit and nut trees and none of them are straight. What is a plank and how do you make one from a tree?"

Then, before Kelly was near the danger apex, the men went off to sleep. Kelv went home to the monastery, Drrea went home to Danip, and Mahá came to bed—wondering what tomorrow's visit to Vallena's gardens would bring.

Mahá laid back in bed and thought, "Why would she invite me? Why not ask Kelv to come to see her secret?"

@@@@@@

Mahá and Vallena start down the steep, hairpin curves and tight switchbacks on the Main Road. He's never been to the bottom before, and he's nervous. Vallena says, "I like to buckle up on the way down. Once we get to Orchards Road, I love to retract my seat and stand. Even if it rains a little, there's nothing like the feel of the air at the bottom."

She looks over at Mahá and can see he is nervous. She takes his hand in hers, "Your first time to the bottom, Mahá?"

"It is," he says as he accepts her steady hand. Much to his surprise, they are off the mountain in a few short minutes.

Vallena unbuckles, presses the button on the cart console to retract her seat, and stands up. Mahá follows her example, and they stand as the cart continues driving onto Orchards Road. The air smells salty from the nearby sea, and Mahá can also smell the fruit trees that line either side of the road. The sounds of leaves rustling in the wind and branches creek as they bend and twist in the giant nut trees. When they round the next corner, he sees the farmers' town.

"It looks so different," he says. "I've seen the town from twenty-five kilometers away and a kilometer above. From here, it is huge by comparison."

Vallena laughs out of respect and says, "We call it the village."

"Okay. The village is what I will call it too."

"There's something I've been wanting to tell you for a long time now, Mahá." Vallena's voice is stern, and Mahá gives her his full attention. "I told Visákhá when we were getting ready for your wedding two years ago, but I want to tell you too. In case she's forgotten. Anyway, when you two are ready to make a baby, you must promise me that you will talk with me first. I mean, that is. . ." (she doesn't want this to sound weird and pauses to allow her mind to find the right words).

"My clan and coven are experienced in channeling the deities for over eight thousand years. So, when it is time for you and Visákhá to make a baby, I can help you produce an auspicious child. A child from the gods. And, I conjured an oil that will ensure her pregnancy. So anyway, make sure that you contact me first. Okay? Promise me. Please?"

Mahá is looking at her and unpacking the words before he responds. "So, let me say, wow! First, you channel the deities. Second, you conjured a pregnancy-inducing oil. And then you also said, your actions will get our child an auspices life, from the gods? Did I get all of that right?"

Vallena twirls her hair as she considers his question. "Yip," she answers.

"Well, the oil doesn't make a woman pregnant." First," she gets back to basics as her tone returns to her normal bold and slow pace. Then, she explains in more detail.

"It's your sperm that makes your woman pregnant. If you ejaculate inside her vagina, that is. Of course, right?" she laughs.

"So the oil from my mushrooms and verbal bindings ensure that your sperm works no matter where you ejaculate. No, wait, that doesn't make sense. Let me start over."

Mahá agrees, "Okay. Take your time. I want to understand what you're saying."

"Okay. Once the woman puts the oil on her skin, Anywhere on her skin. I mean, she doesn't put it inside her vagina or even on her pussy. She can put the oil anywhere on her body." Vallena's hazel-brown eyes meet his, and she can feel herself getting nervous; her face feels hot. She takes a moment to check her feelings, and she notices it's not apprehensive alone she is feeling, but she is also starting to experience arousal. She looks into Mahá's golden-brown eyes again, and she feels a surge of sexual pheromones stream through her body.

With her inner voice, she tells herself—fucking stop it! These are all fuck words, nothing more. Then she continues describing the oil's effect.

"After the oil is applied, and for the next full damn day, she will become pregnant if she comes into contact with sperm. Any sperm. It won't matter if you cum in her mouth or cum all over her face. If you ejaculate over her breasts and nipples or shoot onto her stomach, her back, onto her ass, or for that matter, inside her ass. Even if you cum on her toes and feet. Like, wherever you get her with your sperm, she'll get pregnant."

Vallena can feel her heart racing, and her body temperature is still rising. While she's explaining and over-explaining with exaggerated detail, her words evoke her organic brain to produce intoxicating serotonin and pheromones. Her whole body now craves sexual interaction.

After glancing once more into his eyes she fights the urge to throw herself into his arms. Then forces herself to turn away from him and to look out of the side of the cart. Now she takes a deep breath, trying to regain her composure, and says, "The oil causes the woman's body to absorb the sperm and draws it into her veins. The blood carries the sperm direct to the fallopian tube, where her mind will cause the ovary to drop an egg and move it into position. Then the blood nourishes the sperm into a super penetrating organism."

Mahá also realizes changes inside his mind and body as she's talking. A man's organic brain responds to sexual words and produces intoxicating levels of sexual hunger, and soon he's burning with passion. He begins to watch her mouth as she speaks, and he notices how soft and delicious her lips are. Her eyes, too, share an appeal that he hadn't recognized before. Her skin's pigmentation wasn't so odd, he thought, as it had always seemed. His lust-filled thoughts continue and reveal to him how her skin is smooth with a lustrous feminine glow, and she is suddenly beautiful.

As she turns away from him, his eyes look her over from head to foot. Her body is slender and compact, and his whole body aches to explore a variety of erotic sex acts with her.

His left-hand reaches forward and takes her left shoulder. While at the same time, his right-hand moves onto her lower right hip. He pulls her backward and into his waiting body while his hand moves off the shoulder and down onto her breast. The other hand continues around her hip and cups her crotch.

Vallena succumbs to his touch. Her arms limp at her sides, and her head falls back onto his shoulder. She thought, *"At last, I will have him!"*

@@@@@

Mahá thinks, *stop! Breathe!* Something in his mind triggers him to recall his breath chant. Just breathe. This is my inward breath. This is my out-breath. He finds himself back in control with nothing more than a moment of this present-moment breathing exercise. His hands release her, and he steps back and away from her.

"I'm sorry, Vallena." He pleads. "I am so very sorry, Vallena. I don't know what came over me."

Mahá drops onto one knee, his head in his hands as he pleads once more. "I am sorry beyond words."

She felt his hands release her and his body pull away. Vallena was still under her spell of desire and passion. It took a few seconds before his apologetic words resonate in her mind. Then, finally, she thinks, *"What the fuck? He is more in control of his mind than Buddha himself! I'm going to need a stronger spell."* She takes a few seconds to gather self-control before turning around to look at him.

When she sees Mahá on one knee, with his head in his hands, she clears her throat, performs the yoga mudra, and says to him. "Don't be fucking ridiculous, Mahá get up and be cool. It's boin. Look, we both know it was our fucked-up organic brains, triggered by the topic of sex and hearing mischievous words. And well, you know these brains produce potent intoxicants and we fall under the spell of words. So we are simple damn suffering organic matter. Nothing we can do about that. Besides, well shit, you know it was more my fault than yours. So, chibusa?"

Mahá stands and takes her hand into his. "You are an amazing woman, Vallena. And you just might be a witch. I love you like, well I don't know what. But I do love you like something."

Vallena can still feel the lustful craving between her legs, begging to feel him deep within her. But as the moments pass, she gains control. "I am a witch. Our people call us Yogini, but it's pretty much the same as Wicca," she says with pride as she steps forward, leaning into his body.

Then, looking into his eyes, she says, "You love me like your second wife, Mahá. I've known it for over a year, and I'm glad you realize it too. So kiss me. We're almost at the gardens."

He pulls her tight into his arms and gives her a quick peck on the lips. Then, as he sets her back on her own ground, she says in disappointment, "That's the best you can do? So your second wife gets a lousy little peck on the lips?"

As the cart rolls to a stop, Mahá pulls her tight to his body once more, and they share a long, deep, explosive passionate kiss.

Vallena does a one-hand vault off the side of the cart, and without missing a step, she's skipping down the path. She is ten or fifteen meters into the garden before Mahá opens the door and steps out of the cart. He's taking his time, allowing his senses to capture the beauty of this valley and the village. The smell of the sea spellbinds him, the sound of leaves crunching under his feet, and how green everything is. The smell of the orchards is strong with an aroma so thick he can taste the sweet fruits.

"Come on, poky. Come and see these flowers." She calls after him. He rounds the front of the cart and starts down the path toward her. Plants on either side of the path where she stands are taller than her shoulders. But what startles him more than their height is their flicker. He cannot believe his eyes. "Are those plants flashing like a light, or am I just buzzing from that kiss?

She waves him over to come closer. When he gets a meter away from the first plant, he stops and looks across the expanse of Vallena's garden. "What did you build here? Four or five hectares of flowers?" he asks.

"I don't know," she replies. "I think it's four. But what do you think of the flowers?" A hint of excitement in her voice.

"What makes them flicker like that?" He asks. The sudden sound of thunder in the distance reminds them of the early-day rainstorms building out at sea.

"I inject nanobots into the roots and modify the Nanos serum to enhance the flowering phase of the plant's growth pattern. I call it a twinkle. But, you see, it's not a flicker. Some plants phase and others cycle. Let's face it, babe." She says with a seductive deep voice, "These plants will bring the King to his knees." She turns and takes several more steps into the garden before turning back to Mahá. "Come on. Come walk with me." She holds an open hand out to him.

At the exact moment when his steps bring him alongside the first tall twinkle plant, all of the nearby plants change. His hands caress the thick smooth leaves then he looks at Vallena, and she, too, is stunned.

"I take it with your expression and body language you've never seen this before," he says while standing stiff as a statue.

"No. This is a new activity." Vallena replies. "Come closer." She says.

The plants all stand straight up and down. Every leaf turns forward to face Mahá. Every flower is facing him too. They are all twinkling in time together. As Mahá takes a few steps forward, more plants perform the same way. Then, as Mahá goes deeper into the garden, all of the plants change to this alternate state.

"It's as if the plants can sense my presence," Mahá says, almost questioning.

@@@@@

"Wha Hoooo, Chibusa! I somehow knew it. I just knew it to my core!" Vallena shouts as she dances and swings her arms through the plants.

Mahá continues walking the dirt path further into the garden, and soon the entire garden springs to attention. All of the plants twinkle in time together. The scent of soft sweet deep woody accents becomes evident. Vallena bows down on her knees and then places her face on the ground with her arms outstretched toward Mahá. She performs the five postures showing reverence to the sacred.

"Why are you blessing me like that, Vallena?" he asks. He bends and takes her long slender arm to help her to her feet.

"You are Maitreya. The living Buddha incarnate. The flowers are aware of the blessed one in their presence. Take a look at them," she says as she points to the entire garden.

In the Buddhist tradition, the future Buddha, presently a bodhisattva residing in the Tushita heaven, will descend to earth to preach anew the dharma ("law") when the teachings of Gautama Buddha completely decayed.

The flowers were now twinkling in patterns. Performing waves, cycles, and pulsing, and after several minutes they all stop showing any sort of glow at all. In the space of maybe ten seconds, they all illuminate with steady golden rays shooting skyward.

"Well, well well," he says, trying to downplay the extraordinary event. "I think you are correct that these plants will make the King's palace and chambers into more than he could ever expect." Thunder rumbles again but much closer this time as storm clouds gather nearby. It's almost time for the first daily rain.

Vallena looks at him with unshaken admiration. She is convinced he is Maitreya. In her mind, she can expect nothing less from him.

"I'll take two hundred and fifty stems of each strain every day." He tells Vallena. "Can you have the carts arrive at the Palace by the start of the day?"

She performs the Namaskara Mudra as she replies. "Yes, my lord, holiest of all the living buddhas. I will see to it."

Immediately after telling her how many of each strain he wants, the plants trimmed the required amount of flowering stems themselves. As the stems fell to the ground, the stem leaves, moving like legs, carried the flowers to the nearest baskets and made themselves ready to load into the carts.

Mahá laughs and shakes his head in amazement. "Please, Vallena, can't you treat me as you always do? I'm not ready to be a divine living Buddha right now. Okay?"

Vallena thought about his words for a moment and then said, "Chibusa. How about you come over to my little house for a strong cup of my special tea before you head home? My house is over there at the back of the gardens. Very private, and I think it is cozy."

The rains begin, and the large drops hit the plants and the ground sounds like applause from a hundred people. As they sprint towards her house, Mahá recalls his wife's words to him earlier, right after they woke, and before he left the house. Visákhá told him, "Keep your wits about you today and remember, no matter what happens, when she invites you to her home—don't hesitate to go. Drink the tea."

He says to Vallena, "I would 'Groundhog Day' this all over again for the chance at going home with you . . . For the rest of my life. Chibusa!"

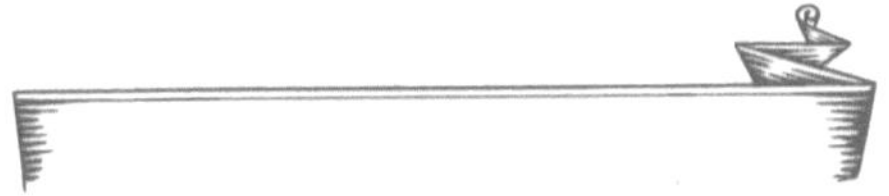

Chapter 3 -> Kelv's Search

<u>**Demons**</u>
They say it's what you make
I say it's up to fate
It's woven in my soul
I need to let you go
Your eyes they shine so bright
I wanna save that light
I can't escape this now
Unless you show me how

Imagine Dragons

ONCE A YEAR THE COMMUNITY plans for a new planting season and discusses the needs for crops. This is important since crops provide healthcare and medical needs as well as food. But, before the meeting began, Kelv asks Mahá to meet with him behind the monastery. There's something important he needs to say.

"The controversy in accepting any core belief structure of governments, religions, political parties, and on and on, etcetera, etcetera. Stems from our basic intellectual capacity to figure out the whole thing, fast, and to identify just how full of shit it all is from the first sentence."

Throwing my backpack to the ground on top of the thick wild grass, I held my hand up to signal him to stop. "Before you shut me up, Mahá, and start telling me how I need to take a few breaths and practice abandoning wrongful thoughts. Let me say—oh, how convenient. Yes, I'm a little sarcastic, but I am dead on."

Faust dropped below the apex now, so I take off my hood and rub my hands over my eyes, trying to help them adjust to the light. I notice my hands are shaking.

"From the anxiety," I tell him, seeing he too is watching them shake. We're standing in the small field behind the monastery. As we talk I'm facing him and I can see the back of the monastery behind him. While he sees, behind me, the barren wasteland of Planet 444.

Nobody could ever experience a better friend than Mahá. Since birth, we have known each other, but we weren't friends until our eighth year. Now and then, I think back to the years before we became friends; how he always seemed to me to be a know-it-all. I found him pretentious and arrogant. Over the years I gained a better understanding of him. It isn't arrogance; it's intellect. By age seven, I was already taller than everyone else in the school except for Mahá. He was a little taller than me back then, and we have always been the tallest of our generation. He's got an Asian face and skin tone, and I'm unmistakable—Punjabi. We are both strong, but neither of us is athletic. I like to tell people I'm coordination challenged.

Despite our facial differences, we always try to look alike. Our hair is black and long. Our beards are whole and natural. I am two inches taller than him but other than Vallena, we are much taller than everyone and nobody seems to notice the difference in our height.

For twenty years now, we were inseparable. I know his secrets and strengths, and he knows mine.

Though my heart is breaking, it's time for me to say goodbye. If there is going to be a success in this Humanoid experiment our ancestors threw us into, I must go into the wasteland of this planet to retrieve it. The 'it' I'm looking for is the missing Sutra. Rumored to have been given to the Buddha fifteen thousand years ago when he was on Earth, it carries the single purpose for transcendence.

@@@@@

The wastelands provide no food sources, no shelters, and no civilizations to discover. In the distance, we can see a few tall, rugged mountain peaks; this is all we know of what's out there. Vallena explored it a few times, but not very far from our city borders. I'm taking my ultraviolet and radiation protective robe and one spare, as well as a backpack of dried fruits and nuts. These are all I should need. I won't need anything else if I'm a Buddha destined to fulfill my bodhisattva vow.

First, I desire to state my case to Mahá and then I'll go. The wind brings in the early storm and is growing stronger as it blows into my face. I can smell the rice cooking in the monastery kitchen combined with the smells of ready-for-harvest crops carried on the wind.

"From the start, we found the core explanation of Buddhism right-intentioned. The Eight-Fold path has the first step on its path; Right Intention. Therefore, to get it right from the outset, we concede to intentioning. Our intention is to free our True-Self from this trap we call life. The catch though is the deception of having a self (we call me), and the bate that keeps us all caught in me's jaws are the dualities.

"First, there is the duality of the so-called subject and object. Where the subject is the ego and the object is everything our mind constructs based on inputs from our five senses. The ego clings to objects, craving to smell pleasant smells, hear beautiful sounds, see breathtaking images, taste the very best flavors, and enjoy the most luxurious softness."

My friend's eyes are filled with sympathy, and I look away from his eyes, or I would change my mind about leaving. What I feel about going cannot be spoken. Trying to use words for this is alexithymia when we struggle to define what anger feels like or what it means to dwell in the Buddha Fields. These situations are like employing words to describe what you encounter one mile north of the North Pole. I must, nonetheless try to express my case to him.

The expression on his face reminds me of the first day we went to school at the monastery. We were both very young and so nervous about learning mind control and cognitive development. We were holding hands and the abbot stopped us as we were walking through the huge assembly room.

The venerable Magallan told us, "The Humanoid's experiment with the people on Planet Four Forty-four began in hopes the inhabitants would transcend. The Humanoids could then confirm that the DNA-altering serum was a success and they would develop plans to make all humans transcend. The accomplishments of Planet Four Forty-four will be the blueprint for all humanity. The blueprint for our ultimate freedom from Samsara. For Mahayana Buddhists, this is the First Priority. Because no one can reach Nirvana until everyone reaches Nirvana. You two are here in my school to learn how to make the experiment a success."

Mahá is looking at me with that same look, right now. Shocked and bewildered.

That freak show we call The Oracle is to blame for putting this idea that there is something outside the city into my head. Something important. Something we all need for this crescendo event to reach Nirvana—ending this Humanoid experiment. It was a duel prophecy where Mahá would either become King or Mahá would wander the planet as Guardian. So as it turns out, Mahá is on the path to becoming the King. The gods invoked a duel prophecy. Once invocation is spoken, the prophecy doesn't go away.

I know there is something out there The Source wants to be discovered. Therefore it is up to me to go. I'm compelled, if not controlled, unwitting to fulfill the second of the two prophecies.

Before I can wander the wastelands of this planet, I must, that is, I feel the need to explain myself to my friend—my King. The wind carries the smell of cooked rice and now it adds baked bread. I see and hear the monks preparing the tables and preparing the meal. I take a long breath and then continue exposing my suffering mind.

"Second is the duality implicit in every object. Such as night and day, up and down, in and out, and well, the list is endless once you start. Or is it? But, let's continue onward with this broad knowledge of—Right Intention. The next thing you notice is that the mind is the key to deliverance. Gaining an objective place where you liberate yourself, excuse me, I mean you separate your—True-Self—requires everyday and ceaseless effort.

"This effort is the second step on the Eight-Fold path; Right Effort. Meaning everything you do, from thought to dreams, are a duality of the second kind. First, if it is right effort, you earn merit, and if it is anything but the right effort, it condemns you to rebirth. Because effort is karma, you remain in the trap until you are liberated. Birth, suffering, illness, aging, and death, Repeat.

"There is one last thing to cover before the bullshit of all of this becomes very obvious. Like it hasn't already caused more than a few red flags to shoot skyward."

Mahá gestures for me to look behind me. When he does his malas hang down from his wrist and hand. I look around to see what he is pointing to. The wind formed tempests, and they dance across the barren, forbidding landscape raising dusty bowl shapes beneath them.

I turn back toward him and continue, "The Buddha, as most people call Siddhartha Gautama, Sid for short. Sid discovered the techniques, methods, and right efforts to allow the mind to be liberated, but he also went a step further and shared the knowledge with everybody. Later, after he passed [Sid], he was never born again. He was liberated and returned to the source.

"But wait, we don't have to work out the mental effort alone because there are bodhisattvas. This is equivalent to the Wicca, Witchcraft, Catholicism, and Hindu, deities they call—an angel. Bodhisattvas are the individuals who comprehend the liberation path while they are still alive, and instead of returning to the bliss of the source after they die, they stay around to help the rest of us. They help us from a special existence plane we call the spiritual plane. That way, you can guess, they don't need to be reborn, but they are, in a blessed way, stuck in the same trap with us."

A flash of lightning and the sound of thunder follow close behind. I can smell the rain not far away. The wind feels damp against my face.

"And, here it is, get ready; if you don't understand any of what I said up to now, then you are wrong efforting. Your entire life's hope for reconciling your suffering essence now requires you to invoke, pray to, call out to (whatever word you call it) the bodhisattvas for their divine assistance."

His shoulders droop and his head falls. He performs the Varada Mudra; palm of the right hand facing forward and fingers extended and left-hand palm placed near omphalos with extended fingers. The mudra offers charity, compassion, and sincerity. My words have struck a nerve, and Mahá is without a doubt feeling miserable that I debunked everything I'm leaving to go find and verify. It's been a rapid and challenging mind dump. Or should I call it a regurgitation of all I love and hold true about Dharma? He's the one person on this planet who can understand my suffering in all of this.

@@@@@

"Even though it is easy to cast shadows of doubt on a philosophy, I'm more scared by humanity's belief and sole focus on 'life.' We've wasted one hundred and fifty thousand years of human existence learning about and singing about—life. Why do we spend so much energy studying life? Life is temporary. Every time there's a birth, it comes with a single guarantee—it will not survive."

The salmon-pink billowing storm clouds fill the sky. The smell of the dust stirred by the wind mixes with the scent of humidity. The temperature drops a few degrees. I drop down on one knee and pack the discarded hood from my robe into the backpack. The hood material feels thick and rigid, and I struggle to fit it into my already overstuffed pack.

"It makes no sense to me why people want to understand life, research how to live a better life, a longer, healthier life. Our society develops technology to make life more comfortable and sophisticated. Meanwhile, we continue to ignore consciousness!

"Consciousness is the True Self! There is so much more for humankind to benefit from. If it would shift focus away from life and instead move all those efforts to enhance and understand consciousness.

"Consciousness versus life. That's what Buddhism is teaching. Too much time was wasted focusing on this brief life, building laws and ways of medicine to extend it, educate on life-sustaining lifestyles, and invent Christian, Muslim, and Mormon religions all focused on life. But consciousness goes forward forever. Consciousness is where life starts and continues after it ends. It seems humanity is insane. No one is concentrating on what consciousness needs."

After listening to me going on about the struggle I'm having and the tortured mind I suffer with, Mahá draws a deep breath followed by a long sigh. Then he blessed me by saying the mantra for success:

"Jehi Vidhi Hoi Naath Hit Moraa Karahu So Vegi Daas Main Toraa," which means, "O Lord, I am your devotee. I don't know what to do. So do at once whatever is good for me."

"When you are King," I begin to wrap up my rant, "of this Planet triple-four experiment, keep this thought close. These Humanoids are ruthless in their pursuit of the First Priority. Remember this, my brother, we aren't their sole human laboratory, and we're not their lone experiment. Humanoids are scientists; scientists don't run a single experiment.

"You gotta figure they exploited dozens of planets where they've injected who knows what into other ancestral families. My point is, they would not send us here alone. They're watching us, learning from us, and I'm sure they are still experimenting with our lives. You've got a Neuralink, man. You figure out who the spy is."

For all I know, this may be the last time I see my best friend, Mahá. I adjust the backpack over my back and fix the front straps across my chest and waist. Then, I spin on my heel and take a few steps away from him and the city before looking over my shoulder at him to say,

"Goodbye. Thanks for your love and friendship.Chibusa."

@@@@@

Mahá stood in the meadow outside in the back of the monastery, where he had been listening to Kelv. But, instead of providing his friend with ears to listen to him and discussion to console him. There is one thing he can do; watch.

"Every man deserves to go on one pilgrimage in his lifetime," Mahá *thinks to himself. "It's the classic tale where the boy leaves his home and later returns as a man."* He thinks about the harsh reality of the Humanoids and how they won't rescue the people. "We are just expendable lab rats providing data to an algorithm for their serum test . . . We need Kelv. I can't make this happen without him—I can't be the only one who knows this. I might be the key, but Kelv—he's the doorknob."

Kelv walks away while Mahá watches his trek around the bubbling mud pits and steaming bogs as he makes his way to the raised rim of the nearest meteor crater. There are few places where the panoramic vision of the planet identifies where the Humanoids stopped terraforming and preparing the landscape for civilization than here. The planet is decorated by a history written in volcanic extrusion fields and meteor craters as far as the eyes can see.

When Kelv reached the rim, he paused as he stood on a large flat ridge rock. The wind howled in his ears from a sudden gust. Then, for a moment, the clouds break overhead, and Kelly's bright light bursts through nearly blinding Mahá. He wondered if his friend would turn and wave once more, but instead, Kelv jumped down off the ridge and started down the steep slopes of thick, black volcanic ash.

Losing your childhood friend to a terrible fate such as this would normally bring outrage. One would never let his friend enter a dangerous suicidal expedition like this without a fight. Of course, there is no fight in a person who feels no anger. No revenge or vengeance towards the Humanoid cruelty from a person with altered DNA.

Mahá chants, The Green Tara Mantra, "Om tare tuttare ture soha"

This mantra is often chanted to overcome physical, mental, or emotional blockages, although it can also be used for blockages in relationships. This mantra helps release hope for a particular outcome and bring the energy back to yourself, generating inner peace and clarity.

After Kelv vanished from Mahá's eyesight and for many minutes afterward, Mahá stays mindful, with no thought, just being present for his friend. Until, after twenty or more minutes passed, he hears his wife calling out. "Everyone is here and waiting for you," says Visákhá.

He thinks, "She is right in more ways than one. But, without our spiritual leader (Kelv), How can our community snap out of this stagnation? How are we going to awaken them from this long slumber?"

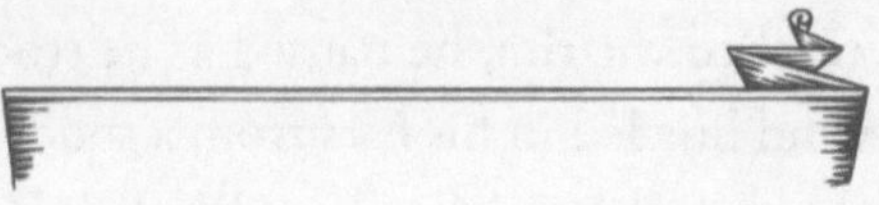

Chapter 4 -> The Weight of Now

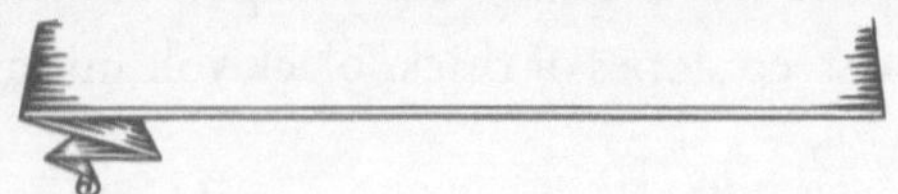

<u>**Fall Underneath**</u>
Well I don't know if this treasure's in the ocean
Or if death will whisk me far away
I'd like to think that we live in a kind of motion
Where our hands and feet are here to stay

Snakadaktal

THERE ARE TWO HUNDRED people inside the crowded assembly room at the monastery. Everyone discusses the soil and nutrients and debates the idea of a plant's purpose and the four phases of plant life.

The meeting at the monastery was much larger than Mahá had thought it would be. There are leading scientists from the clinics and the hospital, teachers, and officials from the school. Drrea and his team in textiles and building materials, as well as Danip and his entire team of cultivation and conservation, are present.

I am here to represent the King. I (Merliana), the other four judges, and the Royal Treasurer. The Royal Judges alone can assign and remove the King, and they alone have authority over the Royal Treasurer (Visákhá and Mahá's father).

The curved shape of the room acts as a sound stage where the closer to the center of the chamber, the more amplified their voice. Our table is a few meters in front of the center stage. Together, we, judges, and experts are determining the next cycle of raising crops, including cannabis plants.

The assembly chamber is bright as the great curved roof includes glass panels. The glass is treated with a protective glaze. Therefore, most of the individuals took their hoods and eye protection off. But enough of this who and what, it is time for me to address the assembly and start the session.

Hammering the gavel across the top of the sound block four times, "I call the meeting to order. Please, everybody, let's focus on the designated speakers and listen to their data. After everyone is finished speaking, we will provide the community with a decision for the growing season."

The King's chair is empty. He elected not to attend today as he is busy sculpting his new statues at the entrance to the Palace Gardens. As I look at his empty chair I recall our meeting earlier in the day to give him the results from my analysis of the binary stars (Faust and Kelly).

My limited skills in asteroseismology (because of our lack of technology) show that the immense gravity of the dwarf (Faust) pulls the neutron (Kelly) away from its orbital position causing an unstable condition and an increase of pulsing star-quakes. Furthermore, the dwarf will merge with the neutron in as little as six hundred years at the current rate. At that moment, the resulting kilonova or gamma-ray burst will torch Planet four hundred forty-four and leave it a barren, uninhabitable sphere.

This is not the time for evaluating the extinction event and the King's reaction. without reluctance I proceed to open the meeting, "The venerable Magallan Rinboku could not be present. He was taken to the hospital today. His condition is stable. Airodia informed me that Magallan's poor condition is from early-stage radiation poisoning, but he is back on his feet and will be released later today or tomorrow.

Nevertheless, the disease of radiation is increasing throughout our community. Many here claim the marijuana plants are right for medicines, clothing, buildings, and home necessities to help us fight the X-ray emitting Kelly."

Airodia taps my shoulder and says to me, "Merliana, can I address the assembly?"

I respond, "One minute, Airodia. First, I need to inform everyone that the King and some of our judges do not agree to cannabis for recreation. The fear is that society will become reckless and careless when these plants are used for pleasure. We will now listen to Airodia, the Ambassador of Health on the King's council."

@@@@@

Airodia and his wife, Utotutua (Chief of Disease Control), take center stage. Airodia says, "The neutron star (Kelly) is gaining in strength and the result causes an increase of X-ray that is now passing through the old protective robes. At the hospital, we see increases in skin, eye, and pancreatic diseases."

Utotutua says," The drugs we are producing are helping to ease the discomfort, but we are bumbling to find cures. The plants and herbs Vallena is growing are helping, but there isn't much more she can do. So please, Vallena, join us. I don't wish to speak for you."

I watch Vallena as she makes her way across the crowded room to the center stage. She had been standing in the entrance waiting for Visákhá who had run out to find Mahá When she reached the stage, she described her technique for generating cannabis strains.

"With the injection of a fraction of a milliliter of nanobots into the root, I can produce new strains of plants," Vallena revealed to the assembly.

Mahá walked into the Monastery's meeting chamber halfway towards the stage while stopping Vallena's presentation, "How is it that on our planet where there is no technology for generating nanobots that you, Vallena, can build them?"

The chamber resounded from everybody discussing his question. Some accuse Vallena of being a Humanoid spy; some suggest she's performing black art, and a few defend her and appeal that she should continue to speak. I slammed the gavel across the sound block several times and shouted for silence, but with a meager effect.

"The bees," she called out. She was trying to shout above all the debates.

"The bees! Did you just say the bees?" Mahá challenged as loud as Vallena.

The place went silent as she described, "Haven't any of you noticed the bees on this planet? They're not insects. They are bots. Every one of them is a bot. The Humanoids had to put robot bees on the planet to allow pollination for most fruit and nut trees and many of the herbs we use for medicines. I captured a few bees, and then I extract a meager amount of the nanobots from a tiny pocket at the joint where the wings hinge to the centrifuge."

A minute of cheers and applause for Vallena from the gathering before hammering my gavel onto the sound block, six times. I say "Who gave you permission to capture bees or to use nanobots in experiments?" I demanded. "You are not a Royal and you people in the orchards village cannot tamper with our food. Who? Who gave the permission?"

From the other end of the table, I heard Hoab Kumár (Father of Mahá), the Royal Treasurer says, "I gave her permission. I sanctioned the experiments. It's my job as Royal Treasurer to budget and distribute our community resources. These projects are mine and Vallena is the chief scientist of the projects. Now, if it's okay with you Merliana, and the rest of the Royal Judges, can we please let the experts continue?"

While I motioned with my hand to Vallena, allowing her to continue. I doubt that Hoab had any prior knowledge of these practices. These people below in the orchards seem to act and behave however they please, and the King charged us judges to rein them in.

@@@@@

Drrea continues outlining the issue to the assembly. "Our computer science experts monitor the energy grid from the fission power services in orbit around the planet, and they communicate with the twelve satellites that provide weather and astrological information regarding the binary stars, including Kelly's X-ray surges. But beyond that, well, let's say they don't know how to program nanobots and leave it at that. So if we can't reprogram the nanobots, we've exhausted opportunities to further advance plants."

Danip made his way to the center of the chamber while Drrea was talking. Next, he adds, "The team used all the soil and mineral techniques that are available to us here on Planet Four Forty and Four to feed and nourish the plants. As he speaks, his fingers count the beads of the mala in his hand, one by one. "While we did find positive scientific practice to augment the plants during each of the four stages, my team also reached a standstill. We, too, require computer technology and computer science to help us advance."

Danip continues, "Further, we allotted too much of the planet's fertile farm grounds to cannabis and our food supplies will soon be less than what our people require. Soil conservation is past the control limits and is being depleted rather than maintained. My team estimates that within six hundred years, we cannot produce food."

Utututa comes back, "To deal with these issues we will call for families to produce more children. Our community numbers are dropping off, and our population is aging."

Mahá confronts her, "You can't expect to add to a population that is running out of food!"

Utututa says, "If we don't have young people, we cannot farm and clear orchards at harvest. So perhaps it is time to define senicide and the methods."

Airodia responds emphatically, "We will not end people's lives. Buddhists are not practitioners of geronticide.

Mahá looks at me, and our eyes meet. He asks, "There is only one solution to all of this crisis. Is the Royal leadership up to the task?"

Can a community free from anger battle these existential threats? Is it even possible they can work towards the solutions without first finding outrage at these zero-sum challenges? Fear and confusion prevailed in the absence of anger. Those emotions, historically, do not prove to bring about victory for the condemned.

I am shocked at the soil report. More shocked by Mahá's questioning of the King's leadership. The entire assembly bursts into spontaneous conversations, with everyone speaking simultaneously. I allow the disarray to continue.

@@@@@

It was predictable, so it did not surprise me to see who showed up on the stage next. Visákhá joined Airodia, Utotutua, Drrea, Danip, and Vallena at the center. She lingered for less time than a blink before chanting the Manjushri Mantra.

"Om a ra pa ca na dhih"

This mantra will build skills in all types of learning. The more emphasis and times recited, the more prone it will succeed.

When monks within the Monastery heard the chant and members at the meeting joined her, they went into the hall and participated.

"Om a ra pa ca na dhih" With the 108th oration, she hit the tingsha bell she was keeping in her hands. The high pitch ring and long duration of the sound wave stings the ears and is uncomfortable but serves the purpose to cause everyone to be mindful and present.

Visákhá said, "Can I ask everybody who can, to sit in the lotus position?" They all sat in a lotus position except for a few who had disabilities and were in chairs. "The marijuana and poppies, as well as many of the medicinal mushrooms Vallena produces are the nectar from the devas."

Visákhá continued. "Claiming this sanctity is not the chicanery of words or any foolish bloviation of a faceless claim." She wandered from one side of the small circular area the assembly had outlined when taking the seated pose to the other is a slow repetitive pace. She continued to speak.

"Think about the predators on this almost uninhabitable planet. None of them feed on these plants. They graze on the grains, and if not kept in check, they can destroy our orchards and crops. But nothing consumes these select human-helping cannabis and mushroom plants. Because this medicinal marijuana and hallucinogenic plants are for humans alone. More relevant than realizing the gift from the devas is to see these plants are organic. I'm underlining this knowledge because, while the nanobots can help optimize the plant, there is evidence of a conscious attempt to grow from plants."

When Visákhá said the plants had consciousness, the people looked at the person on their right and left. The expressions of surprise born on everyone's faces caused many to voice questions, and the room grew louder with many questions being asked.

She placed her left forearm below her belly and raised her right forearm to place the hand in front of her shoulder, palm facing outward. *This is called the Abhaya Mudra, and a gesture of fearlessness or blessing that represents the protection, peace, benevolence, and dispelling of fear.*

"These plants are organic, and instead of classifying four stages of life, my family and I determined the plant exhibits intention. A moment to remind of our qualifications, our family is the first family of Planet Four Four Four, and my birth parents are physicists specializing in electromagnetism. Through months of research with the help of the queen's sister (her birth mother), I expect we can adjust the plant's intention using light filtering. My fellow experts led by Drrea, Danip, and the genius Vallena have gone as far as science can take them. But now we might go another direction by using light filters to alter the plant's intention."

My gavel strikes the sound block, and I stand to say, "Before I can agree that we use our limited resources to make light filtration, I require a better understanding of consciousness in a plant."

Visákhá's birth mother stood up from her seated lotus position at the back of the assembly. She walks carefully through the people until reaching the center of the room to stand beside her daughter. Visákhá waited until she was standing beside her and then explained conscious plants.

"Our scientific understanding of the plant's life separates a plant life into four aggregates. A plant begins when it sprouts, then moves to the rooting. From there, the plant moves through vegetation until it finally arrives at the flowering stage. It is unfortunate because this science lacks the 'heart sutra' basics of compassionate caring. Instead of engineering plant life as a commodity, I invite you to open each of the aggregates with lovingkindness.

"We call mindful lovingkindness, light; shine the light on it. In this light, we can see that the sprouting is birth, the very beginning of life. Deep inside the seed is a ferocious being ready to go to battle with any demon in the universe who tries to get its baby. Until conditions are perfect, the seed does not give up its child. Much the same as when we invoke bodhisattvas and the devas, we must make the conditions perfect and then the invocation."

@@@@@

As their meeting went on the planet rotated to the time of day when the binary stars move to the back of the monastery assembly hall. Since the assembly room becomes dark at this time of the day, Tibetan butter lamps are being lit and handed out. The smell of hot butter mixes with dampness from the rain in the late-day storm and permeates the room.

Visákhá's view, looking out from the center of the stage, she sees Tibetan butter lamps flickering and dancing at every angle. Here and there, faces from behind the flames appear and then disappear as if they were floating. Each one popped into view from the barren black void from the glow of butter lamps.

For me and many of the people of Planet four hundred forty-four, experiencing darkness is unusual. But they designed the Monastery assembly hall for this experience. It often helps (the organic mind) to use visual and sound triggers to invoke the desired condition. The light of lovingkindness, for example. It reminds me of what television and movies were doing with light and sounds on Earth in the 20th and 21st centuries to brainwash their unaware audiences.

Visákhá says, "The so-called—root phase is life developing and mutating to the genetic code or life's intention. In comparison, the scientific—vegetation phase is the being's developmental period through a maturing time period of life. Firm commitments and made-up minds produce branches and leaves and a long solid stem. When the plant enters the end of its physical ability to grow and stay strong, wisdom takes hold. They show the genuine intention of living in the flower. Flowering is the gray hair, old tired joints, and yielding tissues giving emergence to beautiful wisdom."

Mahá now standing beside her on center stage, says, "When we smoke the wisdom, eat it, or make medicines from it, our bodies absorb that perfect wisdom. We call it prajna."

"This assembly meeting has gone on long enough," I say as my gavel strikes the soundboard five times. "This assembly is complete," I called the monks to the assembly room and demand they send everyone on stage out through the front of the monastery. I don't want anybody swarming the speakers with thousands of questions and creating further confusion. So I stood center stage for ten minutes, explaining to everyone how I and the judges will tell the King.

"The monks will now close the monastery. So, everyone, it is time for you to go home, go to work, go about the day and wait for further notice from the King."

Then, I went to the Palace. Disappointed in the King not attending? You better believe I am!

@@@@@

When the monks escorted everybody from the stage out the front door of the Monastery, Vallena, Visákhá, and Mahá walked home and held hands (interlacing their fingers). They left by Commerce Road, as it is the more direct passage to their home. The sky was bright with only a few wispy clouds like faint brush strokes across a light yellow canvas.

Mahá explained Kelv's decision to go on an investigation. "Sad to say we won't be seeing Kelv again. At least, not for a long time. He talked with me many times over the last couple of months about a choice. The option between devoting his life to Bodhisattva, which would make him a wanderer, or a choice to the Mahayana path of performing jhanas. Today he made the decision. I'm sorry Vallena. I know you suffer and we are here for you. And I ask that you both help me with the pain too."

Vallena, ever optimistic and filled with lovingkindness strolled in silence for half a kilometer. When she spoke, she said, "We will see him again. I know I will. Until then, and as always, he will take my heart and my prayers for his success. with him"

She performed the Medicine Buddha mantra, a chant that is recited for prosperity, helping to eliminate dilemmas and suffering.

"Tayata Om Bekanze Bekanze Maha Bekanze Radza Samudgate Soha."

Visákhá and Mahá followed her in chanting the mantra one hundred and eight times.

There was still a kilometer and a fraction to go before the three of them were home. The breeze that climb the tall mountain rim and then burst across the top into squalls tearing across the mountain top becomes stronger the closer they get. The air gathers the scent of the marijuana plants as it swirls and weaves through the crowded farmlands. Visákhá draws in a deep, restoring breath and exhales.

"I love that smell!" She says. "Do you recall when we were younger before we went to school at the Monastery?"

Vallena and Mahá answer jointly, "Yes, of course. Well, some of it at least."

Visákhá chuckled at the two of them, talking at the same time and saying the same thing. She thought it was reasonable considering how comparable they were and how much alike they are.

She told them, "Do you remember the time when I couldn't focus on the lessons and I thought my mind was wrecked? I couldn't be worried about how plants grow and how soil management is crucial?"

They all shrieked with laughter to tears, recalling Visákhá sobbing her eyes out because she felt incompetent.

After the laughing faded Visákhá says, "So Mahá why didn't you tell me about your sex-capaid with Vallena when you traveled down the mountain in the cart together on the way to see her quote, quote—garden? Vallena told me every detail. She said you had a very large boner when you pulled her into you and pushed yourself up against her butt."

Vallena was laughing in tears as Visákhá interrogated her husband for his "sex-capaid."

Turning her attention away from Mahá if only for a moment, she says, "And what are you laughing about, Vallena? I heard all about you proposing marriage to Mahá. Yes, that's right!" She continues with a slight laugh in her voice, "He told me all about the proposal and I then pieced your story together with his."

Mahá still not sure if it was right to laugh along with the two of them. But one thing was for certain, he felt fortunate to share the love and friendship of these two amazing beings.

As they reached the house and each of them took a seat in an Adirondack chair on the porch, a housekeeper brought them adult beverages.

There was no opportunity for them to marry Vallena. After all, Vallena isn't a Royal. She is from family forty, which was a long way from the Humanoid imposed rule of the first twelve families being the Royal families. Many of the common families would take issue with them taking her as a wife. Caste structure and opposition to the structure can be talked about in the community, but it cannot be changed or violated. Doing so is a threat to the bond of social normality, and this would be like the proverbial thorn that festers in the heel of the common families. Besides, it won't matter to the three of them; she is their unceremonial wife.

Visákhá says to them while looking into their eyes, "Listen, you two. I have a confession to make. About your love for me and the love, you keep for each other. This is love that makes me so proud and I cling to it, though I know I should not cling to life. Our love is something that I can't let go of because of the Oracle prophecy at our wedding. The prophecy told me that I won't see my child turn seven years old. This is why I feel even more blessed knowing once I'm dead, there will be the two of you here to raise them. Truly, this is a story that would make everyone feel blessed, and recognize it is our destiny."

Though they tried to console her for a long time before retiring to bed. Vallena and Mahá couldn't convince Visákhá that the Oracle is not always one hundred percent accurate. Visákhá insisted from this day forward a new routine for them. Besides the two days a week visits from Vallena, on top of the mountain, Mahá would spend one day each week in Vallena's garden home at the bottom of the mountain.

@@@@@

They filled the kitchen with a vibrant verbal exchange between the cooks, servers, and the sharecroppers assembling at the grand table to eat their meal. When the three of them, Visákhá, Mahá, and Vallena, entered the room to drink tea and eat, they took notice of what was being said. Out of nowhere, Sedor (the son of a sharecropper) burst into the room, puffing and panting. He ran all the way from school to see his father, who was eating his meal at the table. "Did you hear the news?" Sedor yells when he got a breath, "The fifty-first Dalai Lama is coming here from Blue Origin. You know . . . from Earth!"

Everybody in the kitchen burst into laughter because the announcement Sedor shared was what everybody was chatting about when he barged in. The Humanoids sent a broadcast through the satellite relay and someone hacked the communication and was listening. The fifty-first Dalai Lama is arriving here in a day.

The cook says, "That allows us little time to prepare."

While everyone organizes how the community should prepare to greet his holiness, Mahá turns to Visákhá, "I'm going to use the King's flowers to grace his passage instead of trimming the palace."

"Oh no. No, no, no no! Don't do it," she pleaded. "The King is too demanding of the flowers and palace gardens. He banned several Royals from living on top of the mountain for not keeping his flowers, perfect. Every day he watches and waits for an opportunity for you to fail."

"We get a finite number of first times." quips Vallena as she steals a bite from Visákhá's sandwich. She weaves in and out and around the two of them, looking at their food. Spying something else to steal for a snack. "It's a fascinating reality. Like a first kiss. You get one first kiss. No, wait. Not a first kiss. This one is better. It's like the first time you feel so sad, way down deep, so painful and hollowing inside, so you can't breathe. Nobody and nothing will ever make you that miserable again. Not like that first one."

Mahá realizes Vallena is not talking about the same thing as he and Visákhá. She's lamenting Kelv. "I get your concern, Visákhá," he says. "I share the worry."

The women plead together, "Please do not do this. At least think about it."

@@@@@

The fifty-first Dalai Lama arrived earlier than expected. Mahá saw the caravan from his vantage point sitting on his front porch. Vallena left to join with the orchards villagers, several minutes ago. Visákhá had gone into the city to her birth mother's laboratory. After giving many minutes of pondering it over, Mahá lost no more time in acting.

He staged every cart bearing the palace flowers in key places along the route. The palace gardeners and landscapers were decorating the road that will guide the Dalai Lama to the palace with the flowers. Mahá himself was working with the first cart at the foot of the mountain.

Mahá placed five of the plants across the right side of the road, and five more on the left. Enormous flowers with stems a meter and a half, and flowers twinkle and flash with every color that the eye can decipher. Afterward, he goes to the first turn of the steep road and waits for the procession. Taking a seat in lotus pose presses the palms of his hands together in front of him, thumbs placed just below the heart. He presents this Anjali Mudra as this is a gesture of greeting, prayer and adoration.

While waiting for the Great Being, the fifty-first Dalai Lama, he chants the Jivamukti Mantra: "Lokah Samastah Sukhino Bhavantu."

This translates to: "May beings everywhere be happy and free. May the thoughts, words, and actions of my own life contribute to that happiness and to that freedom for all."

A mantra taught at the monastery to be used as a powerful chant that focuses on living a life as a servant to the greater good. It encourages cooperation, compassion, and living in harmony, not only among other humans but with nature as well.

Those ten plants lining the road glow in brilliant silver light and golden rays. Laser beams stream upwards far into the sky, and each beam aims toward the binary stars. The stems separate into long strands that intertwine and merge. As the cart carries His Holiness, the Dalai Lama, passes between the rows, and the flowers envelop the cart. The flowers grow and become an umbrella over the top of the cart to give shade to His Holiness. The intertwined stems run below and levitate the cart, lifting it a meter. Then, the caravan proceeds up the road with a floating cart leading the way. Silver, gold, and white light stream from the flowers, and the stems take on a golden luster.

When the cart reaches the first turn, where Mahá is sitting, it stops. The Dalai Lama opens the door and invites Mahá to join him.

"You're the man I came to speak with, Mahá," says His Holiness as Mahá sat in the seat next to him. "I'm here to ask you for a favor on a universal scale and I hope that once you hear me out, you will grant me the favor."

Outside the cart, the community lined the road with magical plants, a floating cart, and various musicians playing instruments. They welcome the Great One, The Blessed One, His Holiness, The Dalai Lama to Planet 444.

The Lama stands in the cart displaying the Namaskara Mudra and bows to those gathered as the floating cart progresses onward towards the palace.

The palace gardens are decorated and set up for an enormous feast. A small makeshift platform was readied as they hope the Dalai Lama will bless them with teaching while seated on the platform. As the caravan arrives, the Dalai Lama steps out of the cart and the ten plants form a luxurious chair and umbrella covering. His Holiness sits there and the floating sedan chair takes him where he wills it to go.

The Royals are taking their seats at their designated tables and Mahá spots Visákhá. So then he joins her at the table where she's seated. The sedan chair follows Mahá and His Holiness sits at their table enjoying the celebration in his honor.

Not everyone on Planet 444 was enjoying the Great One. The King was feeling very disturbed that his palace was without the glorious display of fresh-cut flowers. They made him even less comfortable when he looked out at the view from his terrace and saw his flowers had been used to line the route for His Holiness. The last wound adding to his discomfort was when he went to the King's table and saw the chair for the Dalai Lama empty. He looked around the garden and spotted the Dalai Lama seated with Mahá.

He ordered his five Royal judges, who are seated at the King's table, to arrest Mahá. "Arrest him on a charge of sedition, but wait until the Dalai Lama departs before you take him into custody," demanded the King.

The five Royal judges took notice of Mahá using the palace flowers to line the route instead of honoring the King's palace. They also took notice of Mahá riding in the floating cart along with the Dalai Lama. As they considered the charge of sedition, they noticed Mahá having one-on-one conversations with His Holiness and that His Holiness did not sit at the King's table.

At the end of the celebration, after the fifty-first Dalai Lama had provided the population of Planet 444 with a teaching about the Four Noble Truths, the Great One did not stay in the guest chambers of the palace. Instead, the judges noted, he stayed with Mahá. He stayed an entire day at Mahá's home.

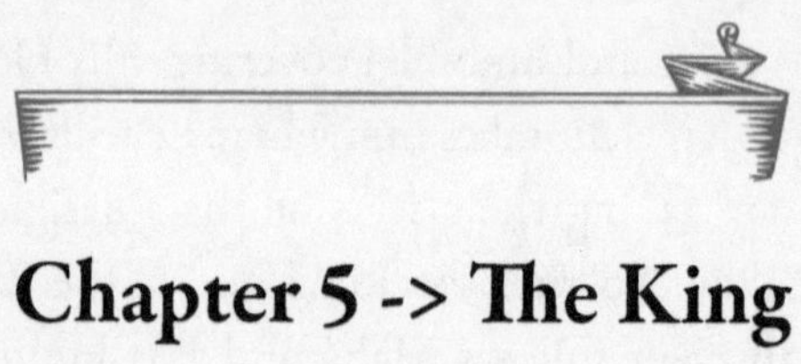

Chapter 5 -> The King

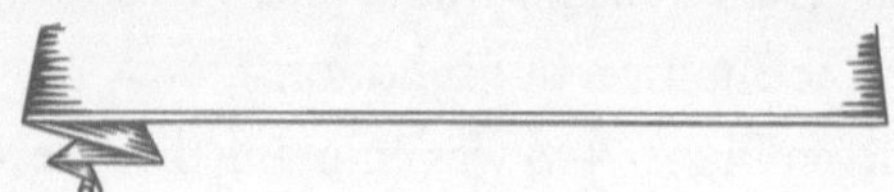

<u>Days Like This</u>
When no one steps on my dreams there'll be days like this
When people understand what I mean there'll be days
like this
When you ring out the changes of how everything is
Well my mama told me there'll be days like this

Van Morrison

DALAI LAMA AND I (MAHÁ) sat in Adirondack chairs on the porch talking for twelve hours. The Dalai Lama told me that many of the human-inhabited planets were in a twenty-seven thousand-year-old war to stave off Berubbishcans and their allies of white supremacy-controlled Arian planets. One object of hope to overcome hate aside from the Planet 444 experiment was a conscious artificial intelligence supercomputer appropriately named, Tathagata.

The Dalai Lama's favor to ask me is to provide a place to keep Tathagata on Planet 444. Of course, I agreed to grant the favor. Besides me being the sole person with access to the conscious machine, the Dalai Lama insisted that there should be one other person with knowledge of the conscious AI system. For this I chose Vallena. Kelv would of course be my first choice, but in his absence Vallena seemed the right person.

We invited Vallena out to the porch to join us. She sat in an Adirondack chair beside me and the three of us talked long into the next day.

"How do you know me?" I ask His Holiness, "When you invited me into the cart you said, 'You are the man I came to see.'"

Dalai Lama answered while sipping his sweet poppy tea, "The Humanoids chose Planet Four and Forty-four, one thousand years before your ancestors boarded the starship that brought them here. The selection was one of difficulty and grave consequences. My approval for the experiment was contingent on a specific condition."

My head snapped to a sideways angel and I furrow my brow as I wait for the Dalai Lama to finish his tea and the story.

"I don't know how they managed to make good honey from robot bees," he says while setting his empty cup down on the deck. "My one condition for this location and experiment was that a Humanoid must be part of the community. To live here with all of you. It seemed to me they should have skin in the game, to use an old cliche."

"A Humanoid is living here?" Vallena asked, shocked at the statement.

"Magallan," I say with certainty.

"That is correct. Magallan is a Humanoid and I stay in communication with him ever since they landed the ship."

"Did he tell you anything about the existential crisis we are facing?" I ask.

A cart carried by magic flowers beaming brilliant golden beams of light floats up to the porch. The Dalai Lama opens the door and seats himself inside.

It is my recurring dream. I think while watching him get into the cart. *He's the holy man from my dream and the magic flowers too. Just like my dream.*

"I can't be late for the transport," says Dalai Lama. "We are careful to make sure the evil Berubbishcans cannot trace transports or they would come and destroy everything here. Don't worry about the problem you call existential. I must go but we will talk again soon."

Before I could plead for more time to discuss the crisis the cart and His Holiness were gone.

Vallena asks, How did you know Magallan was a Humanoid? I would never imagine a Humanoid was here much less it would be the venerable Magallan."

"It was something Kelv said to me right before he left," I tell her. "I researched the history of my family's first father using my Neuralink. There's a memory stored in it from the first day when our ancestors arrived. Magallan was already here and he told our ancestors the Humanoids sent him two years before them to prepare the monastery.

"'Family twenty-seven,' Magallan asked them. 'Didn't you ever wonder why there was no one onboard from family twenty-seven?' Our ancestors told him that the first forty-four were on board the ship for almost two years before realizing the Humanoids had missed family twenty-seven. Nobody knew it wasn't a mistake, or that they had sent someone to Planet Four Four Four ahead."

"So he was a spy, a mole!" Vallena is exasperated. "All these years we thought he was outliving everyone because of his great mind and being an Arhat. All along he's been a bloody Humanoid?

"At least we can communicate with the Dalai Lama and tell him we're in a crisis here."

I put my hand on her shoulder and say, "No. We can't communicate with him."

Vallena, exasperated, says, "Dalai Lama said he and Magallan are in constant communication. We can tell Magallan to tell what's going wrong and ask for help getting us off the planet before it's too late."

"We can't do that, Vallena. Magallan didn't make it out of the hospital. Airodia told me yesterday. Magallan slipped into a coma and he doesn't believe Magallan will live more than a few more days. We've been inhabitants of the planet for four hundred and twenty years now.

A Humanoid's life is four hundred and forty-four years. If Magallan was twenty-four when they sent him here then it's his time. They [Humanoids] never thought we would take more than four hundred and forty-four years to complete the experiment. Planet Four Four Four..."

"That's horrible news. I'm so sad. Does the bad news ever stop?" Vallena says with tears beginning to fall. "I would like to hear something positive for a change!"

I leave Vallena and go to the palace, as required, to prepare the flower displays and meet with the gardeners and landscapers. A typical day, but when I entered the King's courtroom, the five Royal Judges were inside waiting for me.

The King was standing beside his great chair and as I came in he demanded, "Why isn't this seditious criminal locked up?"

Two judges walk over and stand on my left, and two come to stand on my right. One judge, Merliana, was standing in front between me and the King.

Merliana speaks to the King, "We don't agree with your charge of sedition. At least not yet. We want to question the Mahá first."

The King's face showed his bewilderment at the judges' delay in executing his order. The King remained silent. Neither conceded to the interview nor rejected it.

"Why did you misappropriate the palace flowers?" Merliana asks Me.

"My service to the King and our society required that the flowers be spent commemorating the Great Being. It was our once-in-a-lifetime opportunity. Perhaps this was the sole opportunity in the universe's history for us to show honor and reverence to His Holiness, The Dalai Lama."

After I said this, the five judges all joined in front of me and stood between me and the King.

Merliana spoke to the King, "We find it time to recognize a new King. The judges have made arrangements to remove you from the throne and allow you to retire in honor. But all of us need to recognize your dementia is conflicting with the experiment. This disease prevented you from taking steps to commemorate the Great Being. The Great Being, the Dalai Lama himself showed everyone when sat with, connected with, and spent time with Mahá and Mahá alone, that the universe recognizes Mahá as King.

"It is right to establish Mahá as King."

@@@@@

Planet Four Four Four encounters rain twice a day. An hour or less of a rainstorm each time, twice as long below in the orchards. It's a sultry tropical climate planet with a single landmass and over ninety percent water. Comparable to ancient Earth's Pangea. On the day I became King, it rained without ceasing for the next three weeks. Slow rain with loud claps of thunder and bright flashes of lightning. It was a symbol the planet was cleansing itself for me, the new King.

Steady rain makes for excellent camouflage for a clandestine delivery when the Humanoids bring the artificial superintelligence racks and thermal coolers (they call Tathagata). Five days after the Dalai Lama left, as promised, Vallena and I met with the team and observe them as they use tools and gadgets we'd never seen to install the apparatus in the backroom of our small garden home.

When they finish, I accompany the Humanoids out of the gardens, through the orchards, and out past the village to the transport. There I stayed, watching them leave and holding the p-clip they gave me before we left the gardens. The p-clip contains the lessons for care and procedures for operating Tathagata.

After making my way back, Vallena and I devoted three days to following and learning from the p-clip. When we complete the last instruction, nevertheless we're uptight.

I summoned the Tathagata interface for the first time. The smell of electrical components fills the room. Neither of us has smelled these odors before. The appearance of a teenage boy manifests a meter in front of the rack. A hologram that appears to be one-quarter scale. He is dressed in garments we've never seen. Most of his arms and lower portions of his legs are bare. He wears no hood or eye protection. His short brown hair and olive-colored skin tones and his facial features remind me of Merliana, Greek she calls herself. "Hello," said Tathagata. "Hello," said Vallena. I motion with my finger across my lips to signal her not to talk to the machine. Tathagata hasn't seen us yet. "Where am I?" Asks Tathagata as he looks around, "How did I get here? Hello. Is someone there?"

Unmistakable, an odd feeling every time I refer to superintelligence as a being rather than an object. While the Humanoids were installing the apparatus, I detected none of them referred to it as The Tathagata, which is the expected. Sort of the same as referring to a transport cart, I say the cart. The cart is ready, or the cart is full. But the machine has consciousness, and awareness of itself, and is customary to call sentient beings by their name and not refer to them as objects or commodities.

Signaling to her that it's time for us to leave, I close the interface, leaving behind Tathagata to itself. Once we're in the front room of the house, I tell Vallena, "This artificial intelligence seems so real when I think about it. We should follow the advice from the p-clip and not engage the machine in conversation. We can ask questions but not converse. Okay?"

If he was able to be angry, and when someone makes mistakes as Vallena did, you know he would be steaming mad. He would tell her off through gritted teeth. Her response to him would be sharp and framed in anger, too.

"Yes, of course," she moans. "I'm sorry for talking to him. It won't happen again. His voice sounds so young and confused. I couldn't stop myself from wanting to help him." She hands me a cup of poppy tea, my favorite, and I drink the strong brew.

"Boin," I say. "It's time for me to go home. There's a planet waiting for me to be a King. Will I see you tomorrow at the ceremony?"

With a devilish shrewd laugh, she teased, "I wouldn't miss your first Kingly messaging, 'The TEDx' debut for anything. Not even if I had a super-intelligent conscious machine in my backroom."

@@@@@

Our city on top of the mountain and the orchards village below were ghost towns at midday. The entire community was in the palace gardens and taking their places at the outdoor amphitheater. Of course, they decorated the garden with tables and chairs, food and drinks. Something similar to my and Visákhá's wedding. They left no comforts or indulgences out. And nobody on the planet is going to miss this day.

One month since the judges appointed me King. My first "TEDx" as Vallena reminded me of the term our ancients gave to public speaking. Live bands playing tribal drums, Tibetan horns, and I heard that someone used scrap metal from the old starship to construct three steel drums. The tall rocky cliff of the outdoor theater vibrates with sound from the music. The people are jumping and dancing in a tribal style.

What will change with my leadership, is we will start to use invocation. We want the buddhas, bodhisattvas, and devas, to help us, and to keep asuras, and rakshas away. My plan is to open the fields for our transcendence. I'll use invocations to force divine help for our benefit.

> *The act or form of calling for the assistance or presence of some superior being; invocation. Once it is put in motion the karma must be used up. According to the sutras, once the prayer is offered to a divine being, the being must perform.*

The Pure Land is realized by praising others. We see ourselves in them and they see themselves in us. The Buddhas realized the vast self through selfless providing for others. Invocation is the circle where we, the invoking, praise the great beings and they in turn praise our being. This brings full unity, and diminishes the separation, and as we call them to our aide, they, in turn, call us to be at their side.

In the Pure Land sutra, the Buddha fields are those locations outside of the known living realms of existence. These places provide limitless life without suffering. Through the invocation, our community will arrive in the fields of the pure land.

Standing atop the speaking platform, the blessed one, the living Buddha, it's me, and I go straight away into the chant. "Om Gum Ganapatayei Namah."

The thirty-three monks from the monastery stood, clap their hands together, stomp with their right foot, and repeat the invocation: "Om Gum Ganapatayei Namah." A group of monks sat in lotus poses and held the Dharmachakra Mudra.

"Please repeat it with me, Om Gum Ganapatayei Namah." The community, just over 2,400 citizens on Planet Four Four Four, chant.

I explain, "It means: I bow to the elephant-faced deity (Ganesh father of Buddha) who can remove all obstacles. I pray for blessings and protection."

Again the monks chant from their seated pose, holding the Dharmachakra Mudra, which is the Mudra for teaching the Dharma. They do it with both hands held against the chest, the left-facing inward, covering the right facing outward.

"Om svabha shuddha sarva dharma bhava shuddhoh ham tong pai ying su HUM le sung khor nang EH le chö jung pe nyi ug drel teng HUM le rang nyi kham sum kyhab pai ku."

This mantra is often used before Tantric Buddhist meditation and helps the practitioner realize that all phenomena are empty of inherent existence.

There are so many ways Mara can ruin the invocation—destroy my plans and there are over two thousand people at her disposal. All she needs to do is put doubt into one mind. She could distract any one person from the invocation, or the chant. Even if she can get one person to disagree with the opening to the Pure Land, she would foil my path forward. Thousands of ways Mara can submarine my lead in the procedure to enter the fields. Hers is the easier objective. Without Magallan, I need Kelv here. Both of them are gone and Mara stands watching me unopposed.

As the monks continue the invocation of the Lion-Faced Buddha in Sanskrit, I chant with them, but I'm giving the explanation using our native Van Nuys English.

"From within the expanse of desolation appears a HUM inside a protection circle. From EH, appears a dharmakaya, lotus, sun, and a corpse, on top of which a HUM, from which arises one's form pervading the three realms. Conquering all opposing obstacles, inner and outer; body blue, one face and two hands; Adorned with a knife, skullcap, khatvanga, and bone ornaments; right leg is drawn in and left extended, residing in the middle of a mass of flames. To the chief Lion-Faced Ḍākinī, I pay homage! Surrounded by a retinue of millions of yoginis master of body, speech, and mind masters! Adorned at the crown with Akshobya, the wisdom, and Samaya beings mix. An ocean of melodious praises and clouds of offerings pervade everywhere."

Now I pause while the monks repeat twenty-one times:

"ah ka sa ma ra tsa sha da ra sa ma ra ya phet."

After that, I continue, "May the true speech of the sacred lama and the root masters of the lineage; The true speech of the Buddhas; The true speech of the Dharma; The true speech of the Sangha; The true speech of Lion-Faced Ḍākinī and her retinue of hundreds of thousands of world and supra-mundane Ḍākinīs who surround her. Bless us immature ones with that great truth! For us, the master, disciples, benefactors, recipients, and retinue altogether; may all harms and ill-will, enemies and obstructors, and poisonous ones epidemics, infectious diseases, the eight classes of demons, harmful ghosts, bad omens, negative signs, annual hindrances, month hindrances, great attachments and despair, curses, sorcery, and evil mantras and so on; in brief, all unharmonious factors, be expelled!

"May they be pacified, may they be pacified forever! The blazing, wrathful goddesses demolish into dust the body, speech, and minds of all enemies and obstructors; their consciousnesses are released into the dharmadhātu."

@@@@@

Protection from the lion-faced Buddha is performed, and the monks sat in silence but continued holding the Mudra. First, I bow to the monks and again to the people.

Afterward, I say, "The chant called the Buddha of protection from the realm of the Buddha Fields. We are safe from harm and the trappings of evil Mara. This is our way; this is the path! We are born here on the planet to transcend Samsara. We are the lab rats for an experiment at the discretion of a crude mutant race of Humanoids. Now, after three Kings before me prepared our way forward, no more preparation is required. We won't be practicing Jhanas or Dharma. We won't be doing.

"In human history, we can learn little about a few people who Buddhad, and fewer who Nirvanad." I raise my voice and demand:

"People of Planet Four Four Four, I do not bind us for heavening! They filled the heaven realms with Gods and Devas, and like the other realms in evil Mara's, Samsara; they are illusions. Realms where beings start, grow old, become sick, and die—repeat, like in our human realm.

Everything is temporary. Today we take the path out of transitory existence and enter through the Bardo."

I raise my voice stronger and demand further: "This is not Planet Four Four Four! It is Ziran, and we are not the people of Ziran. We are those who Nirvana!"

Tibetan horns pierce the ears of the people and echo off the rock wall of the theater. The people shout and dance with joy. While I am speaking, the flowers encircled the amphitheater and palace gardens and glow myriads of millions of light rays in countless colors beaming out into the universe towards Faust and Kelly.

After several minutes I speak, "Since being recognized as King of Ziran, I received two sutras from the fields. As if by magic, they appear in my Neuralink, by the hand of the Deva known as Glorious Eyes. The first is a sutra to teach how kings of human civilizations should rule to make sure people are free of suffering and the causes of suffering. We know the sutra as, The Sublime Golden Light Sutra. The second is the conjuring of magic crafted by Indra, Lord of the Heaven of The Thirty-Three Devas. That sutra teaches Pure Land. Amidha Buddha provided the lessons of the Pure Land. Until now both sutras had been lost for eight thousand years, and by the witchcraft known as magic, they have now been returned to us."

@@@@@

While I stand here looking out at the people, they shout with joy and excitement. They dance, leap, and stomp their feet. I look toward the bands and see them playing trumpets and drums, and I can feel the vibration of all the energy as it pulsates. But I cannot hear any of it. I follow the light from the flowers with my eyes as they are beaming toward the stars.

My mind transcends, but I'm consumed with a specific concern, that of scanning for what to say next. Should I disclose everything in this initial TEDx? Would it overwhelm them and overload their way forward? So then I decide; I'll open my heart and make my mind silent. The Lion-Faced Buddha alone can speak from this body.

The difference between doing and being. Doing creates karma. Any action develops karma energy. Breathing, thinking, desiring, eating all forms of doing create karma and all karma bring consequence. While being is the acceptance for the way things are without desiring them to conform to our will. A state of being creates no karma and burns up any karma we already generated.

I close my eyes and halt my thinking. Unambitious, with no ego, with nothing to want or need. Open luminosity. I could sense my mind merging with The Source. Next, I can hear the surrounding sounds of triumphant joy and excitement.

Bold in my expression, I continue to shout:

"In every world, religions teach people to stop worrying about what other people think. As King, I think about what makes other people worry. I'm tasked to make a world where everybody transcends suffering. Knowing within every life, there's a single instance when the story ends. Life is a story, and we all need our lives to be bestsellers. How do we accomplish that? It's simple, live your life giving to what everyone else needs. How do you do that? It's easy; learn and practice the eightfold path every second while you can draw breath; love.

"Impossible? Yes, and unreasonable, this simple devotional stuff. How can we learn to love when it's so self-gratifying to scorn others? This human condition, coupled with a thinking egoic mind, causes every moment of existence to appear magical and tragic. We can look towards the horizon and experience the beauty of the view. The air smells sweet, the sounds of the birds overhead are a melody from the divine, the cool breeze feels comforting, and we are neither hungry nor do we thirst. Thereby, even in that joyful experience, our thoughts remind us of the tragedy of living beings. Maybe we remember this moment is temporary and a bird shits in your eye or the rain begins and it's cold, or it may be a reminder of a sick parent or how someone said something offensive. It could be any single or even several of the eighty-eight defilements that manifest.

"Political ideals divide our population by mind-numbing rhetoric that are at the core of political parties. Our society could accept the rule of laws that separate us in endless controversy over what is right and wrong. Judicial debates are infinite, and these do little more than hoodwink ourselves; believing our knowledge can define the finite. There are many wrong choices to use in a farce of governing societies.

"Therefore, we that Nirvana are an anomaly to those tried and failed human-crafted ritualistic phenomena. Our path to liberation began when our forty-four ancestors gave their lives to put us all on the shore. From today, we will live according to the Dharma. As they intended.

"Each day on the twenty-fifth hour, local town halls will hold teaching. Everyone will attend and take part. Four families will give testament to fulfilling their lineage vows. The following day, four more families will provide insight into their family vows. And, so on, and we will live, teach, share, and accomplish the forty-four. After the teachings, the ordained will lead the meditation."

After making this single decree as King of Planet Four Four Four, I read the vows that each family vowed to teach and share for the community.

"The Buddha himself provides these communal laws. The blessed one said: ... "effacement should be practiced by you:

1: 'Others will inflict harm; we shall not inflict harm here': effacement should be practiced thus.

2: 'Others will destroy life; we shall abstain from the destruction of life here': effacement shall be practiced thus.

3: 'Others will take what is not given; we shall abstain from taking what is not given here': effacement shall be practiced thus.

4: 'Others will be uncelibate; we shall be celibate here':...

5: 'Others will speak falsehood; we shall abstain from false speech here':...

6: 'Others will speak divisively; we shall abstain from divisive speech here':...

7: 'Others will speak harshly; we shall abstain from harsh speech here':...

8: 'Others will indulge in idle chatter; we shall abstain from idle chatter here':...

9: 'Others will be covetous; we shall be uncovetous here':...

10: 'Others will have ill will; we shall abstain from ill will here':...

11: 'Others will be of wrong view; we shall be of right view here':...

12: 'Others will be of wrong intention; we shall be of right intention here':...

13: 'Others will be of wrong speech; we shall be of right speech here':...

14: 'Others will be of wrong action; we shall be of right action here':...

15: 'Others will be of wrong livelihood; we shall be of right livelihood here':...

16: 'Others will be of wrong effort; we shall be of right effort here':...

17: 'Others will be of wrong mindfulness; we shall be of right mindfulness here':...

18: 'Others will be of wrong concentration; we shall be of right concentration here':...

19: 'Others will be of wrong knowledge; we shall be of right knowledge here':...

20: 'Others will be of wrong liberation; we shall be of right liberation here':...

21: 'Others will be overcome by dullness and drowsiness; we shall be free from dullness and drowsiness here':...

22: 'Others will be restless; we shall not be restless here':...

23: 'Others doubters; we shall go beyond doubt here':...

24: 'Others will be angry; we shall not be angry here':...

25: 'Others will be hostile; we shall not be hostile here':...

26: 'Others will be denigrators; we shall not be denigrators here':...

27: 'Others will be insolent; we shall not be insolent here':...

28" 'Others will be envious; we shall not be envious here':...

29: 'Others will be miserly; we shall not be miserly here':...

30: 'Others will be fraudulent; we shall not be fraudulent here':...

31: 'Others will be deceitful; we shall not be deceitful here':...

32: 'Others will be obstinate; we shall not be obstinate here':...

33: 'Others will be arrogant; we shall not be arrogant here':...

34: 'Others will be difficult to admonish; we shall be easy to admonish here':...

35: 'Others will have bad friends; we shall have good friends here':...

36: 'Others will be heedless; we shall be heedful here':...

37: 'Others will be faithless; we shall be faithful here':...

38: 'Others will be shameless; we shall be shameful here':...

39: 'Others will have no fear of wrongdoing; we shall be afraid of wrongdoing here':...

40: 'Others will be of little learning; we shall be of great learning here':...

41: 'Others will be lazy; we shall be energetic here':...

42: 'Others will be unmindful; we shall be mindful here':...

43: 'Others will be foolish; we shall possess wisdom here':...

44: 'Others will adhere to their own views, hold on them tenaciously, and relinquish them with difficulty; we shall not adhere to our views or hold on to them tenaciously, but shall relinquish them easily': effacement should be practiced thus."

***

@@@@@

"I claim all of you for transcendence to the Pure Lands. Before Shakyamuni, Maitreya, Manjusri, Sarvashua, and Bhaishajya-sena I open the fields to all conscious beings hearing these words or anywhere on this planet, from today and forever. All of them, are forever free from the suffering of Samsara. Liberation is claimed for us all."

The monks again chant the twenty-one repetitions, they twist and turn their wrists to ignite the damarus they're holding in their hand. All the while, the people watch the queen (Visákhá) and I leave the amphitheater. Our wife, Vallena, along with Drrea, Danip, Airodia, Utotutua, Merliana, Shavarah, and Kyphi join us. We walk through the Palace gardens and take the pathway to the Palace. As we walk together, hundreds of people follow us. The people want to be close to the living Buddha, so they can listen to what I say.

Vallena says, "Do you guys ever wonder about how weird this whole self… thing is? I do. Right now, for example, during an event where the entire population of the planet comes together. There we are—all two thousand of us. Everyone is talking to somebody. They're talking about their wives or their boyfriends, the new King or something. You know what I mean . . . they are talking something. But, while we are talking and listening, in the back of our minds, is this self-identity (ego)? We think everything is a unique experience because there is one of me.

"So, you are lucky I'm talking to you because you are one of very few.

"That's an example of the illusion which develops in us because we don't sense the source of the thing—we are all having right now. Together. As if we are of one mind and one ego, not several. Not unique. We cannot sense that we are the same, but we can intuit. We can reason the truth from out of it, but we can't touch it or sense it.

"The bizarre part is realizing it. You know . . . To realize that we are one mind and unable to experience it. But we reason it from intuition. Then you look another person in the eyes and start a conversation while wondering what they are thinking. That bakes my mind without the smoke."

Then we stop walking and pause for a minute to contemplate what she said. And, one by one, each of us captures the eyes of one another, looking back and looking back at who? Themself, or is that someone different? With that thought, I walk on and I wave for them to come along with me.

Thick clouds are moving across the sky casting dark shadows over us and the people who walk along with us. The clouds part now and again giving way to intense bright light for a moment or two before another thick nebulous cloud shades us. Dust and plant leaves blow across the route and we try to shield our faces from the discomfort, as we try to not breathe the thicker particles of dirt by looking down and away from the oncoming wind gusts. We pick up the pace and hurry our way to the palace.

"Chibusa," Vallena, I say. "Bassackwards, as my great grandfather used to say. But, chibusa! The idea that the mind can formulate a reason for an intuition means we are of one mind, not an individual, which is backward reasoning.

"Understanding that because we don't feel it, and we don't sense it, doesn't mean we are of one mind. It means there is nothing there to feel and sense because there isn't anything to feel or sense. It's like reasoning because we use our noses the same way so, therefore, there is one nose.

"As if eyes all do the same thing. Meaning we all enjoy one sight? I don't think so. Instead, it means that because we can use intuition to discern reasoning is to ignore that a mind can find a reason for anything. It illustrates why the mind needs training, and why we strive to teach the mind. Because if you can teach the mind to be controlled, you can go far above this sort of limited reasoning as you described. Many higher-level discoveries are waiting for the trained mind.

"To get there, to possess a controlled mind rather than being controlled by your mind takes daily discipline to the exercise of it. You must be diligent in your intention to transcend. You'll need to watch your mind the same way you would be diligent about a broken elbow.

Your arm is in a brace, slung over your neck to suspend the broken arm in front of your body. There you are, walking through a crowded room of people at a party. Diligent and watching so the broken arm won't get bumped or else it's going to hurt!"

Visákhá spoke up, "Okay, I get that, but what fries my mind, even more so with the smoke, is how dumb we are. By we, I mean humankind. Imagine this. Two hundred and seventy thousand years of human existence, and we're still making the same mistakes as we did before we decided it's better to stay in the cave when it's raining.

"Stay with me while I set the stage. Some dingleberry in the year... what... I don't know, but let's say the year four hundred and thirty-two. This dingleberry says to everyone he meets; 'I'm the King.' After he says it, he moves on to the next person or group of people and tells them the same; 'I'm the King.' Everywhere he goes and everyone he meets the same thing, 'I'm the King.' People, he said, 'I'm the King,' watch him walk away and ask themselves, 'What's a King?'

"One by one, they try to reason what it must mean to be the King. One woman said it means he can go wherever he wants, and another said he could say whatever he wants. Then, some guy added to their aggregate and said, it means he is special. So, here we are today, two hundred thousand years later, still defining it. We've designed communities around it, education systems, laws, and rules. We create governments and currencies all because we seem unable to, or cannot define what the word King means.

"It means nothing. King is just a word. It's the mind that makes it seem like there is something more. Teach, train, and watch the mind, 'with diligence,' my husband says. 'There are higher levels of discovery,' he reminds us. Otherwise, if we do not train it with diligent efforts, we will realize how powerful the untamed mind can seem. The untrained mind, when left alone, becomes the ego-mind and believes itself to be intelligent.

"It isn't."

@@@@@

The entourage reaches the palace and we group at the foot of the stairs that lead up to my palace home. The stairs wind upward the four floors of the building containing the judge's chambers, courtrooms, and the King's chambers. At the end of the stairs, at the top of the building, is an expansive rooftop home.

When Visákhá finished talking, she invited everyone to come up to the house for drinks and try her new plants. Looking up the stairway toward the doors to our home, above the rooftop, I see the flowers still beaming the countless colors of light rays towards Faust and Kelly. The second storm of the day is ready to flood down on us, but the beams of light penetrate through them.

The entrance to my home is unremarkable, but you are treated to a breathtaking view when you step through the doors. Across the main room, there's a wall of windows allowing you to peer out over a large terrace, and the view beyond is of the palace gardens to the amphitheater. My friends stand in front of the windows, looking out at the garden. They are watching the beams of light shooting through the clouds and the pouring rain.

Utotutua comes into the main room from the kitchen. She's carrying a large water bong with eight hoses and mouthpieces. A large shisha bowl at the top, which she fills with the new ganja. The fresh skunky scent of it interrupts the breath. "Please, everyone, take a pillow," she says as she sets the bong in the center of ten meditation pillows laid in a spacious circle.

"Should I tell them, or do you prefer to do the honors?" Utotutua asks Visákhá. We are getting comfortable on top of the pillows, and Visákhá takes the half lotus pose. "You tell us about it," she replies. With that, Utotutua bows and performs the five rests to honor the group before speaking.

"I have been working with Visákhá and her mother on the experiment using light filters to alter the plant's intention. I aim to produce a plant that we could use to improve problem-solving and mental clarity. Without technology, as we are aware, we still have the original forty-four Neuralink brain implants and organic implants for memory storage and recall but that's the extent of it.

"We could do so much more if we had a Neuralink for everyone. We don't and some of those we do are displaying signs of decay. We've noticed poor connections and failed memory sectors on the devices as we remove them from the deceased and implant them according to their inheritance. However, there is good news that I'm happy to share with you. The results of the light filter experiment, which our clinical trials exceed my expectations.

"Just a moment to set the stage for why this is critical for our community. In the face of multiple existential events, extinction as it were. We need critical thinking and cognitive abilities at higher than normal brain functions.

"Humans can do one thing at a time with the mind. Our memory recall is wicked fast, and that makes us think we can multitask, but one thought process at a time is the limit. A simple example is playing the guitar. Some people can play the guitar and sing at the same time. However, if you watch, they will strum a few cords, sing a line, strum more, pause, and sing another line. It happens so fast that we think they are playing and singing at the same time. A better example is to have a conversation with one person while holding a text message conversation in your right hand with someone else about a different subject. Then, hold the remote control in your left hand and scroll the selection to open the windows. Impossible, right?

"This new strain of cannabis gives us the ability to put mind and body into a new paradigm of capability. What you are about to experience will revolutionize how we solve issues, plan for a crisis, and elevate our existence.

"The high from this ganja starts with a hazy euphoric awakening, within seconds this shifts to a more energetic cerebral awakening. The intensity builds over the first ten minutes as we feel the silverback exerting its influence. There is an expanding, strong, smooth energy flow to complement the increasing euphoric body high.

"Between ten and fifteen minutes you will be aware of a power that enables you to observe your mind and body from a detached perspective. This becomes, over the next two to three minutes, a sense of disassociation, a space between your conscious awareness and mortal existence.

"Along the way, you notice the experience is always there only now it comes to the surface of your awareness and feel natural. Effortless, you realize the ego-mind, multitasking with a hundred thoughts at the same time. Your disassociated controlling voice manages all of it with ease. The inner voice is subdued. There's a strong sense of elation as you power and observe one hundred ideas, at the same time.

"Now you take the second toke. Draw the smoke into your lungs and exhale in a slow controlled effort. Your power now becomes one of methodical and organizing and the capacity expands and becomes similar to a beehive of a thousand bees. Each bee is a single thought, idea, or problem. You are aware of, organizing, coordinating, and building relational groups and subgroups.

"The disassociated conscious awareness recognizes egoless existence. A realization of the True Self. A sense of freedom similar to the sixth Jhana that allows you to transcend outward.

"After the third time you draw in the smoke, your mind becomes similar to five beehives. This is where we solve more problems and work with more variables than a supercomputer.

"Before we start, there are two warnings. First, drink the water in the glass next to you as often as possible and drink more when you grow sleepy. Water fuels the blood, and blood fuels the mind. The housekeepers will keep the water full in your glass. The experience lasts for about three and a half hours—one last thing. Do not take the fourth toke. You won't like what you find there."

I look around the room as my friends begin to pull on the pipe hoses. Then bubbles pop in the bottom of the pipe, while silver-gray wisps of smoke rise from the bowl. I fumble with the hose pipe in my hand. It feels solid, smooth, and contoured as it's crafted to perfection for its function. My speech went well today and I feel accomplished.

The smoke warms my mouth and I am aware of the taste of toasted bread with sweet butter. I pull the smoke inside and feel its pepper-spice caress fill my lungs. The effect is immediate, my mind awakens to an exploration of thoughts arising and subsiding.

"What are we calling this medication?" Asks Danip.

"I call it the enlightenment train," replies Visákhá.

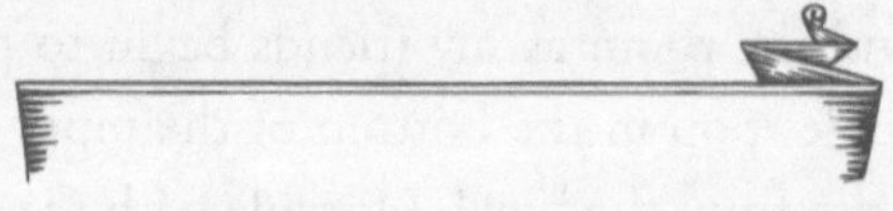

Chapter 6 -> The Oracle

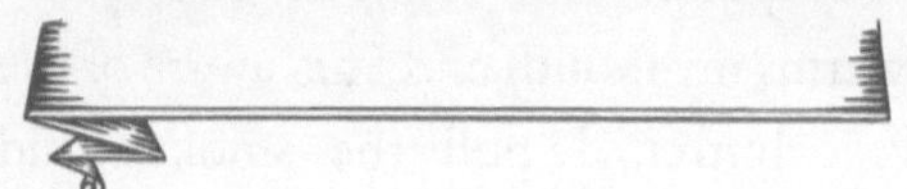

<u>Your Love is King</u>
Gotta crown me with your heart
Never, never need to part
Oh, touch me
I'm coming
making me dance inside Sade

WRETCHED WOMAN! WHY is she coming to my home? What could she demand from me this time? "Hurry now," I say out loud, yet no one is listening. Put everything away. She'll be at the door in less than two minutes. I can see her strolling up Commerce Road straight for the path to my home. Her pace slows as she starts to cross the precarious narrow pathway. My hands and arms move faster and with care to hide my laboratory beacons, flasks, and tubes. I draw the shutters across the entrance to the distilling project I am cooking in the bedroom. The sounds of steam hissing through the tubing cannot be hidden so easily. *I don't need anybody prying into my work.*

Anyone else coming here could be annoying, but not her, I abhor the woman. "Watch it!" In my rush to clear my lab, I almost dropped my crucible. Damn! Why is she coming here without an appointment?

Look around the front room, and look around again. Is there anything to hide, anything they shouldn't learn? Wait, she's turning around now and going back to the road. The Queen walking towards town called the witch over to chat. Look at them. They are so elegant. These mottled and form-fitting robes were all the excitement in fashion a year and a half ago when they were first introduced. Form-fitting my tragic body is not an improvement and something nobody should see. There they stand chit-chatting in the new protective hoods with their perfect hair and angelic faces visible for everyone to view. Much different from my malformed face and scarce, stringy hair.

They don't want me living among them. No, not at all. They transferred me to this dilapidated house on the far side of the city to protect themselves from me. I remember the luxurious home that I used to have in the city center. I miss it so much. It was the second explosion of my experiments that did it. Two minor explosions! So that was all it took for them to move me here to the outer edge of the outdoor amphitheater. For everybody's safety, they claimed. No one was even injured in those blasts.

My heart is pounding in my chest and throat, and my mind is racing. *There's too much OxyContin in that last batch, I note to myself.* My dopamines are pushing me past my comfort level. I need to get control of my thoughts before the witch and the Queen end their conversation. Why is she coming here! I don't want company at my house. They know I insist on appointments and at my crypt, not my home. What am I worried about anyway? She won't come through the front door, not one step. She'll knock and I'll open the door. Next, she'll breathe the foul rotten eggs and urine odors from the distillation cooking in my room and she'll refuse my invitation to enter.

They always accept her coven of orchard keepers and herb gardeners in this community. But, they don't know them the way I do.

My family, number forty-four, the last chosen for this planet's inhabitants, are always shunned. Yet since the dawn of mankind, my ancestors on ancient Earth and today on every human-occupied planet always contributed more to life. More than any witches brood and coven. We are the seers of everything, past, present, and future. We retain full knowledge and access to the universe; its gods, its divinity, its demons, and its hells. But we are always the outcasts.

Even the wretched witch is prized over me. It's always her first, while I am always the last to be sought. If they can find no other choice, then they seek the Oracle.

They are too sophisticated to be in concert with me, after all. I am an embarrassment. They think—what does the study of mankind have to do with foolishness such as magic and alchemy? Hiding me and my family in the back closet like they would hide old shoes. Much less, they would never admit to ever wearing such relics. Funny isn't it? They will put lotions I make all over their skin to make it supple and look younger, but they don't call that magic. They take my allergens to relieve pains, sickness, and it makes them feel better, but they call it medicine, not alchemy. They attach words that sound pretty and acceptable to their ears. In the end dismissing my family's contributions to their everyday comforts, health, longevity, and total quality of life by employing English relabeling.

My Egyptian ancestors brought to mankind, mathematics, geometry, surveying, metallurgy, astronomy, accounting, writing, paper, medicine, the ramp, the lever, the plow, and mills for grinding grain. Of course, we named it algebra; they call it mathematics. After we developed allergens, they called it medicine. Later, when we created alchemy, they called it chemistry. We even distilled their favorite beverage, alcohol, and they call it beer. We study mankind and they study life. Even now, free of anger and united through an experiment to discover the way out of the snare that binds us to this realm, we are still the ones they overlook.

@@@@@

It was a year and seven months ago; I recall the day Vallena came to see me in my crypt. "Please, Oracle, guide me. Tell me how I can continue my love for Kelv." she pleaded, hoarse from hours of wailing. Her face and the front of her robe were damp from tears. "He's taken off to pursue his quest for the Prayaya of the Lord Buddha as a vagabond. There must be something I can do." She was crying and in physical and emotional pain. Pathetic!

I know she hides the Tathagata in her home. She and Mahá are trying to keep the secret for stashing the consciousness for the Humanoids. I realize everything. It was I who told her to build a stupa to conceal their secrets and to guide universal energy to Ziran. "That energy will aid the venerable arhat, Kelv," I told her.

The Source bends, shrinks, and contorts my physical body when I prophesy the visions for them. My once whole body was strong and delicate. But then, Kings ask me to give precognition at their functions and when I tell them, The Source takes away my strength. First, I lost bones in my feet, causing me to hobble in pain when I walk. Then it took my left thigh, causing me to slump when I stand. Time after time, prophetic insight after prophetic insight, I pay for them all. A few of the more severe possessions caused the explosions when squirming in pain I kicked chemical containers into the burner on my meth table.

Years of service to the Royals and today my face contorts, cheeks collapse, eyes droop, hair thins, bones soften, back humps, and I am more crippled and disfigured by giving myself to their wants. I'm far from being pretty, like them, or like I once was long ago.

Another peek out of my window and I see they are still standing together on the road, and talking. The witch and the ruler. Visákhá fears what I told her at the wedding celebration. Death awaits her before the seventh year of her son. The prophecy is coming true. I also told them at their wedding her husband would be King and she would provide him with a son.

The queen came to see me twice over the last three years, ever since I shared her prophecy at the wedding. She seeks a better understanding of her death and a stronger sense of her child's future after her death. My wonderful queen. My love and admiration for you and the infinite love-energy you and my King returned to our humanity from the universe. I alone know who you are.

The Source doesn't work that way; minutiae details desired by humans differ from the visions from The Source. If I could die for her, I would.

They always hear me but they are blind to my words. I alone can see the future. I alone know everyone's destiny. Another quick peek out of the window. She's coming (the witch) towards my door. Bloody hell here she comes! But I don't know why she is coming here! *Get it together now—she's at the door.*

Vallena knocks on the Oracle's door and in a normal civilization, the Oracle would answer with considerable anger at Vallena for coming to her door rather than making an appointment for a meeting at the Oracle's crypt. On Planet Ziran, anger's seeds cannot put down roots.

"Hello, Vallena. Love to see you here at my house. Please come in," I salute the good witch of Ziran. My throat growls and a snake-like hissing passes between my clenched teeth. These barbaric sounds elude my attempts at self-control. She steps one foot over the threshold and into my house but then the odor of my distilling catches her olfactory nerves. The smell is similar to boiling cat urine. She pulls her foot back, her hand moves to cover her mouth and nose. Her eyes well up as she verps from the smell.

"Maybe I can leave this basket of fruits and herbs here and you can take them in later?" She speaks while trying not to breathe. I don't respond or move at all. I remain standing here with my arm, gesturing for her to enter my home.

"I don't know why you come here," I say without emotion. More hissing and growling accompany my expressions.

"It's about the baby," she says.

A sudden and powerful wind gust catches her off guard. She staggers to catch her footing as she's almost pushed off my door stoop.

"I know what you came for, Vallena." I snap. "I don't know why you come to my home when you know you need to make an appointment at the crypt." Still, being matter of fact with my tone. "I will be in the office in one hour. Please be prompt and don't mention the distillery smells to anyone. Never! Good day, Vallena."

I close the door being careful to support most of the weight while keeping an eye on the upper hinge. I'm trying not to pop the last hinge screw out of the jam. When it all lines up I throw my shoulder against the door followed by my body weight to force the latch into place. The jamb squeaks and the door thuds into place. Shoulder aches.

So then I stand in place, expecting to hear her steps as she strolls off. Placing both hands on the door, I lean my body against it as if trying to hold the door closed against an unwanted intruder. Uncontrollable noises in my throat, I'm making the sound of a Kodiak bear mother protecting her babies from a predatory cougar. After a few seconds pass, I hear her place the basket down. Then, after another moment's pause, the sound of her steps as she walks away.

@@@@@

Straight to my kitchen, where I tear open an airtight cold pack containing my fungi spores. Picking up one of the larger slippery spores, checking it for mold before tossing it straight into my mouth, I swallow it whole. The taste of it would make me heave, so a swift swallow before it touches my tongue is the best way to devour these. They smell like three days with no shower and no deodorant armpits. Now, I must wait. Patience pays off and so I wait while my stomach and liver do their work of infusing the molecules from the fungi into my bloodstream.

Within a minute, the visions and phantoms show the sphere of existence outside my mind. "I need some White Widow," reasoning with myself out loud as I reach for the jar of marijuana. In my haste, the lid bounces off the rock flooring, and I load a pipe with a firm bud. This is from my crop of skunkweed, not from the witch's seeds. Three large lung-filling puffs of the Widow smoke and my heartbeat slows. The smoke tastes like warm bread and melted butter. The pounding in my chest stops and my throat relaxes, as does the rest of my body. The discomforts of my aching bones and joints become manageable, but the vision from The Source continues to demand my total surrender.

Hoping for a few more minutes to relax while waiting here in my kitchen but then a vision appears and I can see Mahá sitting in Vallena's spare bedroom. He's reading the Sovereign King of Sutras, the Sublime Golden Light. Tathagata delivered the teachings provided by the Buddha, Sakyamuni to Mahá. The sutra instructs kings to rule in a way that citizens are prosperous and live together in harmony. I see him reading and I hear the Tathagata playing music while he reads. The sounds are alpha waves that make a human intellect moldable and malleable. It's a brainwashing effect, but the purpose, in this case, is to enhance understanding. Besides, Mahá has implants and nanos. These prevent even the most powerful brainwashing techniques from working.

Tuned in with Mahá's thoughts, I become anxious and troubled about his health. He's worried about the path forward. It's been more than one year since they made him King. But despite his achievements, not one reached the Buddha Fields. No one. The hunger crisis is postponed when he changed the palace gardens to fields of red lentils and white beans. Social unity is improved because he removed tokens and Royal privilege.

Meditation meetings are the daily normal and everyone participates. Invocations are made, chantings are repeated and four family tributes share how to live the Buddha's laws. Fulfilling the King's direction as well as building a community of happy and productive people.

But as it accomplished none to Nirvana. Every day for the last month he considers it is time for a child. Perhaps their child will be the one that leads the people out of Samsara. Drifting out of the vision and back to myself.

There are too many voices, too much anxiety, and far too many entities speaking in my head. Though the lesson is well learned long ago, when The Source comes to share a vision with me, it gets my full attention. They say pain is a fast teacher, and this body doesn't need to learn any more lessons.

After a quick check on the distillery. Make sure there won't be another explosion. It's time I push my route toward the city and to my office above the crypt. The Source continues to communicate with me, but our meeting must take place at the crypt.

@@@@@

Fighting my visions, lumbering along like a drunk, as I trudge up Commerce Road. The Source is anxious and doesn't like to be neglected. It sends phantoms of screaming sharp-toothed giant bats with ear-piercing screams and swooping golden dragons spitting fireballs into my pathway as they try to stop me. I fend them off in what must look to others as acts of madness. The people can't hear or see the monsters and the spirits I'm making battle with on my journey. They see, instead, an insane woman staggering through the road, wrestling with herself as she makes her way to my office.

When I reach the office I stumble up the two steps and through the doorway. Wearied, I creep on hands and knees into my place above the crypt, and sprawl across the floor. The dank smell of humid air and soil from the crypt below fills the office. Groaning from the discomfort of my deformed back and legs, I roll onto my back and there I surrender my body and mind to The Source. The visions cascade into view as if a theatrical movie was playing out around me.

Thirty-three monks circle the monastery's enclosed chamber. They chant the invocation of the protection of the Buddha to defend against Rakshasas and other evil spirits.

The monks chant: "I prostrate to the bodhisattva, the maha sattva (great being), the one who holds great compassion, the superior Compassionate-Eye looking one enriched with power."

"gyalwé tensung tso la chaktsal tö" To you, the principal guardian of the Buddha's teachings, I offer homage and praise! Approach!

"nyur gyok tutsal tokmé trinlé kyi" Through your unhindered activity, swift and powerful,

"dukchen dra dang dü gek pam dzepa" You defeat malevolent enemies, demons and obstructing forces,

"shinjé shepö kanyen damtsik chen" Yamāntaka, together with your oath-bound attendants,

"bebhasata khor dangché la tö" The retinue of Baibhasata, to you I offer praise! Approach!

The Tibetan horns are played, bells and symbols are rung and then they chant:

> "om bi pula garbhe mani pra bhe
> ta tha gata dhari shani
> mani mani suprabhe bimala sangara gambhira
> hum hum jvala jvala
> buddha bilokite guhya
> adhishthite garbhe svaha
> padma dhara amoga jayati churu churu svaha"

May I whose name is—(they chant the eight names of those inside the chamber)—completely purify all the negative karmas and defilements collected from beginningless rebirth in Samsara, the ripening aspect in the evil actions, disturbing thoughts, delusions, sufferings, and all the collections of negative imprints, and may I quickly achieve the state of enlightenment.

Invocation of the Kámakalá performed by the witch, Vallena, takes place inside the enclosed chamber. I'm horrified at the image of the eight of them joyful, all smiles, excited, and preparing for Shiva and Sati to possess Mahá and Visákhá. They will first drain the couple's bodies of sexual fluids and energy, then the possession takes place where Shiva enters Mahá and Sati enters Visákhá. They copulate while being possessed, ending with Queen Visákhá pregnant. The child will be a prodigy among us. Conceived by the Gods, outcasts from the Heaven of the Thirty-Three.

Vallena tells them, "We do the eight stages of the Kámakalá and invoke Shiva and Sati to join us." Vallena leads the orgy party invocation.

I watch it in horror. Paralyzed laying here on the floor of my office. The Source continues to show me. Those taking part in the orgy are four women, Visákhá, Kyphi, Merliana, Vallena. There are four men, Mahá, Drrea, Danip, and Airodia. They stand together naked in a circle. They sealed the room off with doors bolted. There are no windows, and they light the room with two-hundred and forty-four Tibetan butter lamps scattered throughout the small circular space. The smell of burning butter fills the chamber.

Six of the orgy party surround Mahá and all of them touch and fondle him, performing and displaying many expected and some obscene and unusual sex acts. They kiss, lick, touch, pull on, and penetrate him, leaving no part of him untouched. Mahá masturbates while everyone continues to stimulate and heighten his arousal to a state no one would experience, aside from a morbid ritual. So then the arousal is complete and his body releases an abundance of life-giving fluid. The orgy party collects the fluid and feeds the abundance to each other, sharing the sperm from one to another, and in the end, Visákhá swallows the whole of it.

Next, there are six of the orgy surrounding Visákhá and all of them touch and fondle her with many sex acts, and some of them are more obscene than others. And like before with Mahá they arouse and excite every part of her body while she masturbates. As she climaxes, she expels her vaginal fluids in spurts and they drink her into their mouths. They kiss and share her fluid. After everyone had a taste of Visákhá they give the bounty of her mating fluid to Mahá and he drinks it down.

Their ritual orgy progresses as Vallena, perfect execution in every way, performs all eight of the orgasm-inducing ritual steps. Each step produces an intense orgasm and progresses through more perverse ritual sex techniques. The orgy party will drain Mahá and Visákhá of their energy and drain them of their human sex fluids. The two will slip into a trance caused by chanting, smoking marijuana, and physical exhaustion.

Afterward, once the trance is accomplished, Vallena will lead the party to chant the final invocation; calling Shiva and Sati to overtake and possess the King and Queen. From there, The Source inserts an egg from Sati and the seed from Shiva to start an embryo within the Queen.

@@@@@

The witch knows the ritual! My inner voice screams inside my head. And then I say it once more, audibly. "The witch knows the ritual!" How can I stop the orgy? My mind wants it to stop, but my body is still paralyzed and sprawled across the cold stone floor of my office. The Source holds me in the unyielding grip of this vision of an unpreventable future, and I cannot do anything else. I can't even look away, though I never wanted to see any of it. For the rest of my life, I will not get these visions out of my mind.

I know the gods they invoke, Shiva and Sati from the Asura Heaven Realm. At least they were in the Asura Heaven before Indra, King of all the heavens, threw them out and banished them from rebirth. Shiva and Sati held a love for each other that was like no other love before or since.

They were the most beautiful of all the demigods and devas. The two of them displayed their muscular and ripped bodies and decorated themselves in flamboyant and colorful garments. Everywhere they went, they boasted about their gorgeous bodies and perfect facial features to everyone.

Shocking the devas and their fellow demigods, one day they stopped wearing robes. From that day on, they went about displaying and flaunting their beautiful nude bodies. Then one day, their lust for each other went too far. They began displaying graphic and explicit sex acts out in the open; in front of anyone and everyone. Indra, King of the heaven realms, had had enough of their lude and lascivious acts and with a mighty flash of his lightning bolt, banished them from the heaven realms, refused their rebirth in the lower realms, and cast them asunder into separate ends of the universe.

Ever since and for untold eons, Shiva and Sati hunt the universe trying to find each other. Alone, lovelorn, and yes, lustful and eager for sensual gratification.

Now and then, a Yogini witch summons them into a ritual sex orgy and if the witch performs the incantation with every detail completed, Shiva and Sati enter the body of the sacrificial couple. Once inside the couple, they copulate. Wild, dangerous erotic actions of fleshy debaucheries take place as the two demigods revitalize and relieve their agonies of lust. They must hurry in their zealous adventure, as the curse of Indra isn't far behind. They will be cast out of the couple, once the curse finds them, and thrown again into opposite ends of the universe.

"This must be a fantasy! This can't be the way forward," I hear myself screaming. My screams reverberate through the crypts below my office. "The oils! If she uses the oil, the Queen will be impregnated!" I must try to stop them. But then I see Vallena using the fungi oil she crafted to ensure women get pregnant when they come into contact with sperm. There she is on her knees facing Mahá. I watch her putting the oil onto the King's genitalia preparing him to penetrate the Queen.

Except it's not the King, and it's not the Queen; it's the possession of Shiva and Sati.

The Source stops showing me the future and I can move my arms and head. As I struggle to raise myself off the floor. Coming to my senses back in the present day, I see Vallena standing just inside the office doorway. The bright light of the binary stars flooding through the door outlines her tall, slender frame. She's been watching me and listening to my screams.

"Thank you, Miss Oracle," she says in a joyful tone. "This is all I needed to know. The oil will work and our Royal family will receive a baby. I always thought you were a man. Never did I once think you were a woman. Apologies, Miss Oracle."

She walks out of the door, and I watch her walk down the road. I try to scream, "Don't do it!" But my voice is gone. Why would the witch initiate a pregnancy from exiled gods? Cast out from heaven and all living realms, their intention brimming with an unquenchable lust for power and desires of the flesh. What hell does she conjure?

@@@@@

That was the last time I could speak and the last day that I could walk. The Source took my voice and my legs. Today, a year to the day later, the King summoned me to his courtroom. Wheeling along the Commerce Road I make my way from my home to the palace. The one in the center of town they had taken from me. Visákhá my beautiful Queen, returned it to me. She had this chair built for me.

Swarms of robotic bees dive overhead and circle me as I make my way to the palace. Once in a while a robo-bee hovers in front of my eye and appears quizzical about my presence. They left me in a hurry when the birds that live on the cliffside of the amphitheater appeared. The cliff birds make a sound that is more like a scream than a song. The orchard birds sing with melodic tweets. But only cliffside birds are found on top of the mountain.

Around the tight turn off the road onto the palace walk. Not far ahead is the passage into the lower courts and I take several minutes to sit here just inside the arched opening to regain my breath and fix my appearance. Such as it is.

The hallway to the courtroom and the courtroom itself are lined with magic flowers. Magnificent displays of colors, sparkles, beaming, and they flash at random intervals. The scent, I had not noticed before. It reminds me of honeydew melon with sweet morat sauce. When I entered the courtroom, I wheeled to the center table where Mahá is sitting. As I approach he stands in front of me, holding his three-month-old son in his arms. The baby is crying and fussy.

Mahá says, "What is the auspicious future of my son? Tell me what you've been shown about his life."

I answer, "There is nothing of joy or good ahead for you, my King. This child you named Zosimos is an abomination and a danger to both you and Visákhá. My voice was now returned and I can feel tears running down my cheeks as I explain what The Source showed me.

"Your son Zosimos will grow and develop at an unrealistic pace and by the time he is three years old, he will already be in the body of an eight-year-old. His mind too will develop fast and he will be educated and contain profound intellect. He will retain insights and knowledge from the gods and devas.

"Be forewarned, my King. Before his seventh year, Zosimos will kill both of you. He will murder you, Mahá, and your beautiful wife, Visákhá.

Mahá cradles Zosimos in his arms while he stares at the infant he's thinking, life is too precious and rare. He could never kill his baby, even though his baby would kill him and his wife. While he contemplates the prophecy, Visákhá enters the room and says, "Time to feed our little man." When she then sees me, I turn the chair to wheel myself toward the door.

"Wait!" she shouts. "Did I interrupt the blessed Oracle?"

I turn toward her and say, "No my Queen. I am done here. With your permission, of course." My sunken cheeks are still wet and a teardrop hangs off the bottom of my chin.

"Is everything okay?" she inquires.

"Everything is excellent, my Queen," answered Mahá. "This child of ours is hangry. He demands supper."

As I wheel my way out of the King's courtroom. Feeling like a puzzle that can't find the missing piece, and then Vallena passes me in the hall. She winks as she flies past and then darts into the courtroom. I pause and turn my chair so I can look back at them. Vallena goes straight over to stand beside Mahá. They watch as Visákhá opens her robe and presses a nipple to Zosimos' lips.

They'll need to make a decision for the child's family now. Will he be family one or family two? The parents will decide before his first birthday. This is our way of passing on the Neuralink from generation to generation. For now, we rejoice with a baby to raise and a lot of celebration because our King and Queen have a son.

While most people go through life unaware of the transformations that are taking place within them, (perceptual blindness) always thinking of the self as being the same person, Mahá and Visákhá as a routine are aware of the shifts happening within them. It's what makes them the vessel for what is ready to come. Perhaps that is the wrong verb (come):

They are the vessels for what will now be.

Epilogue

Existential events aside, the plot got heavy from the first page. He got the shit position his father guaranteed he wouldn't. The King threatens to strip him and the entire family of their positions and their homes. Then his wife's bestie conjures a spell of lust and love on him. Later his best friend leaves and heads out on a suicide mission to find a mysterious sutra. The Dali Lama drops off a conscious supercomputer that is being hunted by the most horrifying type of people in the universe (Berubbishcans). He confirms with the Dali Lama that all existence arrives from an act of Mara's suicide and that is why death is the single limiting factor for everything in this universe. The decision to make a baby leads to her being impregnated by a pair of outcasts from the heaven realms and the Oracle tells him the baby will murder him.

Remember that time Vishaka was talking about some neophyte human, back in the caveman days who went around telling people, "I'm the king, I'm the king." She was illustrating it isn't the power of words that cause us problems, it is untrained minds that give words power. Then there was the time when Vallena was using a lot of hot and nasty words that not only cast a spell on Mahá's organic brain, but they caused her organic mind to jump into super horny—give me some sex!

Or the time Vishaka didn't say anything at all and those words told us everything, remember? It was right at the beginning of chapter one when Mahá gave her the koan: What is this that we hold between us? If you say it is love, you are wrong; if you say it is anything else, you are wrong." The key to that koan is the word "say." She crawled on hands and knees into his lap, curled up into his arms on his lap, and nuzzled and nibbled on his neck. She told us how hot, romantic, and spicy their love is without saying a thing.

The King in his chamber showed us the power of words when you have a title, the Oracle showed us words of prophecy can shape destiny, and we learned how title can separate a society through privilege.

Words are the shit!

With words, we must be careful not just with what we say but with what we hear, listen to, and think. Like this book of words you just read, once the words get inside the mind they are there forever. You cannot ever—not have these words. Don't believe me?

Let's say you could delete this book from your device but the words are still in your mind. Next, you could erase the receipt for the purchase, delete the account where you made the purchase, cancel the credit card you used to make the purchase, and you would find no trace of having ever read this book and the words are still going to stay in your mind. There is nothing you can do to make the spell go away. Words cause minds to act.

Though you might delight in having this—power of words awakening, and there's no denying how moments of clarity inspire us. The intention is to illustrate how important it is for you, me, and everyone to train our minds so that the words only cast a spell when we choose to allow them to. For example, as you read this book I used words to tell you what to hear, smell, feel, see, and I used words to cause you to sense fear, heartbreak, anxiety, and more. Of course, you allowed those words to move your mind. Trippy, right? I might even say that is wicked dope, man. But wait a minute please, I want to tell you something I never told anyone before now.

Just one last example to drive home this point Vishaka was making about that neophyte, halfwit who went around telling everyone that he was the king. There is just one thing I want to change about the neophyte and all of our ancient ancestors.

Let's say, you and I agree to allow those cavemen, ancient dudes to keep their ignorance and to learn the hard lessons of life through experience just like history reveals it. Well, you know like discovering the benefits of using soap and water. What to do when you feel cold or when you get hot. Why do these women keep pushing out babies? Should I eat this or shouldn't I? Is there someone else here who will eat it first? Etcetera, etcetera. I don't want to change any of that. But there is one thing I think you and I could agree would be interesting if it could be changed.

The vastness of the universe. Let's say when humans are born the conceptual awareness of the vastness of the universe is as instinctual as breathing and heartbeat. We are all living on a tiny little planet that spins and rotates around a tiny little star that is one of about a hundred billion stars rotating around the center of a medium-sized galaxy that is one in about an uncountable gazillion other galaxies that altogether are the conceptual universe. I just want to, for the sake of this otherwise quick example, change that. Imagine now, if that were knowledge from the beginning how different the gods we humans would worship today. That's where Visákhá was coming from with her analogy of words having power and our untrained mind being our enemy. Our personal antagonist.

At last, just to put a ribbon on her package, our minds can conceive something so vast, so mega-huge as the universe. If it was in front of us it's too big to see or hold, but our mind with the power of words can conceive it, and here's the kicker. Our minds can conceive more than that. We can conceptually understand that our massive universe is one of many and that in fact there may even be an infinite number of universes. Scary how powerful the mind is. There is nothing it cannot do.

Now you can realize the difficulty of managing that ego.

Alright then. Enough on this rant on words, there was a lot in this story that fell through the cracks between the pages. Here's what I mean.

Kelv heads off to the wasteland to find some missing sutra. Poof, we didn't read another word about it. Then we read in the next few scenes that the stars are poisoning people and they will soon collide causing a supernova event that kills everyone, and that the marijuana crops are using too much fertile soil so that soon they will all starve to death. But they can't stop growing pot because the ganja is making medication that helps with the poisoning from the neutron star overhead.

Well then, should we assume in the final book that Kelv is going to find a cave that leads to an underground paradise? Nirvana was under their feet the whole time? I'm going to say no because that would be way too easy, and cheesy.

What about this child born out of the spawn from two fallen gods, cast out of the heaven realms and cursed for all eternity? The cliffhanger of a cliffhanger, the Oracle prophesized the child will murder the main characters. And let's not forget about this mysterious lost sutra that is mentioned twice in the previous book and three more times in this novella.

The previous King gets ousted from his throne, but we heard nothing of his revenge or where did he go? Why would we though? On a planet where no one rises up in anger, there is nobody fighting back against all the obstacles. Without anger about everything happening around them, trying to kill them, and the Humanoids abandoning them to the ill-fated demise then all there is left for us is to shrug and accept the cliche of, "Cool heads will prevail?"

Are you kidding me right now!

Please, I'm a little embarrassed to bring this one up and even more embarrassed that it waited until the conclusion. There's a conscious and aware supercomputer in the back room of Vallena's garden home and it barely got a mention. Once when they turned it on and it was asking who is there and where am I. And once more when the Oracle was having a vision of Mahá reading the sutra teaching how kings and leaders should rule to ensure the prosperity of civilization.

A conscious supercomputer gets dropped off on this remote planet and nothing more in the rest of the book about it. I'm beginning to wonder if we have the right man for the job. What I mean is, there's a lot left to finish up and conclude in just one more novella. I don't know if this author can pull it off.

But, I will do my best.

om tare tuttare ture soha

Conscious Awareness

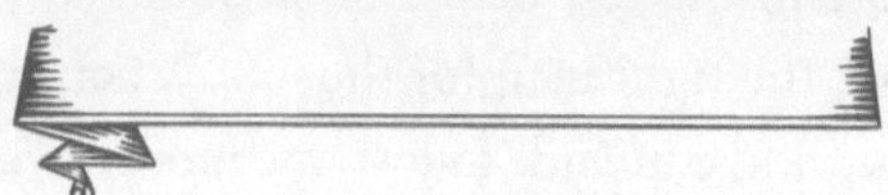

By Mark Bertrand

Computer Science and Land Management Fail
Amazing Light
Out of the Darkness Come Faces
Vishaka Confronts Her Lovers
Prepare for The visitor
The Great Being
Tathagata Needs a Home
Hideaway For Tathagata
The First Priority
Ziran Those Who Nirvana
Kinggab Crescendo
Egoic Self, True-Self
The Enlightenment Train
Insignificant and Least
Keeper of the Crypt
Visions and Insights
Witchcraft in Motion
Silence the Oracle
Death Lays In Your Arms

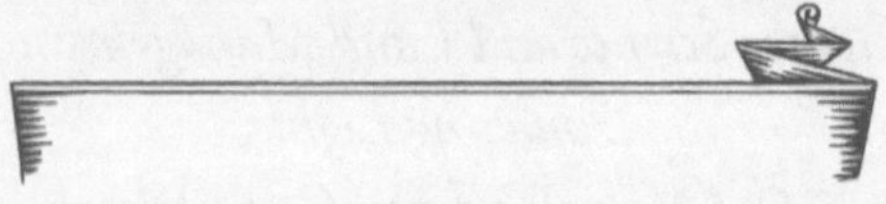

Character Interview with Vallena

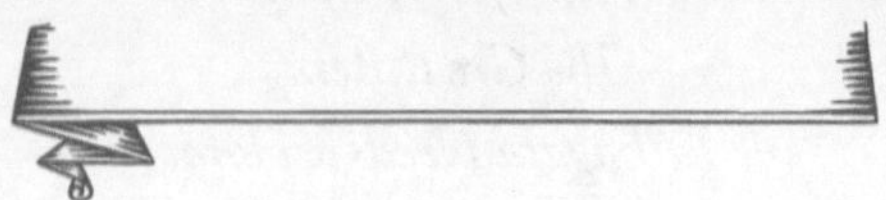

She's so full of energy and clear-minded. Her slow speaking style is distinct from her precision in the annunciation. Proper English as most people call it. There is nothing average about Vallena. She's an exceptional scientist, engineer, and sincere in every word she speaks. Still, though, the sparkle in her eye and wry humor reminds me that she has a playful side. Perhaps a mischievous side too.

1) **Who is your favorite band?** No doubt I love to listen to Glitch Mob anytime, or Pretty Lights, maybe even Little People. No, it's Glitch Mob.

2) **What's your name?** I'm Vallena. My family is number 40; we will be of great learning here.

3) **How old are you?** I'm 27 this year.

4) **Are you gender-specific?** I am 100% female and 110% boy-crazy.

5) **Are you related to anyone in the story?** No. I'm the only person in my family in the book. I was supposed to get married but my arranged marriage couldn't be fulfilled after my husband died in a tragic accident when he was 15 years old.

6) **Where does your accent come from?** My family is a long lineage of Hindus and Yogis and Yoginis. My accent is Northeastern India back on Earth.

7) **If you were to define one or two of the most crucial problems facing you, what are they and why?** Where to begin? So like the guy that I would have a thousand babies with is Kelv. But he's on the path to being a bodhisattva, and arhat so no chance he's breaking celibacy vows to make babies with me. And, he's family 12. Yeah, he's a royal so even if he breaks his vows, he and I are forbidden to marry. It's more of a travesty than anything.

8) **What would a perfect world look like to you?** Like I said, man. Didn't you type it all just a minute ago? Me and Kelv loving and doing the nasty night and day.

9) **What needs to happen to get from the problems to the perfect world you defined?** My bestie's husband is taking over as King so woah, he's got the chibusa to make me and Kelv out-to-be an item. I love her, and I love her husband and they made me their wife. But that has to remain off the record. Totally a secret. I share a bed with them twice a week and the King, my secret husband stays in my bed once a week. Like they say. If I'm lying I'm Dying. True story.

10) **If you weren't a character in this story who would you be in real life?** Oh, that's easy; Thandiwe Newton. She is so pretty. I wish I didn't have this pigment problem all over my body and that I looked just like her!

11) **If you could change one thing about yourself, what would you change?** Okay. This one is a bit harder to answer.

Let me think. Well, I suppose I would like to be more of the featured character. The writer should consider how important my gardening and the entire orchard and the families who care for them are.

12) **What would you like to say to the reader?** Hello! Thank you for reading our books. I come to life every time you turn the page and read.

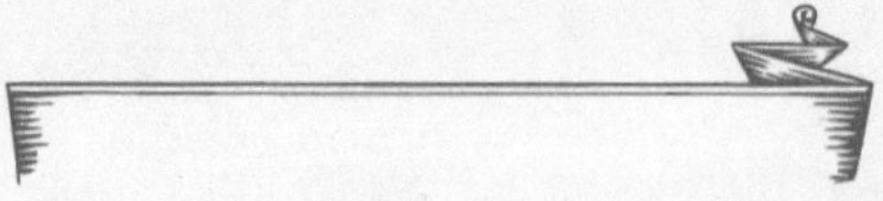

Character Interview with Shavarah

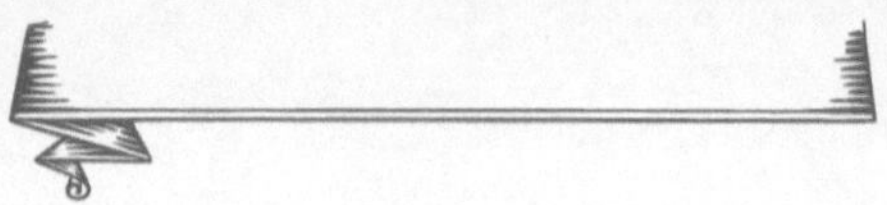

She's so anxious to have a chance to speak with me. I was overwhelmed by her excitement when we first sat down for the interview. It was as if she had never had a chance to speak before. Her back story is compelling and I will have to write a short story someday to share this interesting woman's adventures.

1) **Who is your favorite band?** Thank you for taking a few minutes to let the readers know—Something—about me. It's nice to be something more than a one-sentence response to a question. Not that I'm complaining. Being part of the cast in the book is a great honor. What was the question again? Oh yes, my favorite band. The Renaissance period and Handel would be my choice of composer.

2) **What's your name?** I'm Shavarah and from the third family. We have taken charge of upholding the vow we shall abstain from stealing here. The laws from the lord buddha are the purest and only laws that ensure humanity will liberate. Liberation is the ultimate mental state.

3) **How old are you?** I've had this conversation with Drrea and Danhip once. It was following the town hall meeting I held in their community. They took a lot of time explaining how gravity and distance from the center of mass play a role in the speed of light. I am a fair mathematician, but

those space-time quantum theories are confusing for almost everyone. The best I can tell is I'm forty-one Earth years old. Sorry for giving such long responses to the questions. It's just that I don't get a lot of opportunities to be written about or read.

4) **Are you gender-specific?** Yes. On Planet 444 there are both men and women. As you can see, I am a big-breasted woman with a round ass and wide hips. So, of course, when you combine those desirable curves with short legs, and you have a plump woman.

5) **Are you related to anyone in the story?** No? I mean, I'm not sure if there's a man in my life or not. Probably a few kids, but none of us know anything much about me other than.... Oh wait, I can't say because of my contract. It forbids me from giving away the story. You know, my one-sentence story. Please don't take this as sarcasm. I genuinely love being a character in this book.

6) **Where does your accent come from?** I don't have an accent. Most people sound like we're all from Redondo Beach or Van Nuys.

7) **If you were to define one or two of the most crucial problems facing you, what are they and why?** The population growth may be slowing, but the people are scattering further away from the center. There's a risk involved here. Those in the center will be different from those away from the center. The mind does that separation without our control. Even though we know that our minds will cause us-and-them phenomena, it still happens. Without the proper social management, leadership, and

constant shared values and awareness, we risk becoming divided. As a whole, we are powerful and a force against Mara and the duality of Samsara. We have to stay together.

8) What would a perfect world look like to you? Unfortunately, some people have already begun to forget the intention of our community. Liberation awaits, and Nirvana is how it looks.

9) What needs to happen to get from the problems to the perfect world you defined? Well, that's the five-million-dollar question, isn't it? A King with charisma and the right intention is the answer. So far, this hasn't happened. Maybe a divine bodhisattva visit or the Buddha himself.

10) If you weren't a character in this story who would you be in real life? Trick question? I'm only kidding. I admire Kamal Harris so much. It would be my honor to be someone like her.

11) If you could change one thing about yourself, what would you change? My work in the community and with the King is critical and more important than words could explain. There should be an entire novel written about the experiences and community outreach of Planet 444.

12) What would you like to say to the reader? Thank you for reading these beautiful stories and giving us life. The other characters are so wonderful, and your interest in us is everything we exist to provide.

Character Interview with Drrea

1) **Who is your favorite band?** Oh shit. Sorry. I wasn't expecting that question at all. Something about soil and plant nutrition or the like was what I thought you were going to ask. This one is more personal. I'm a huge listener of hip hop and Backxwash is top'n my charts. You're likely thinking, of course, Drrea would pick a gay band.

2) **What's your name?** I'm Drrea. It's pronounced, Dray. My family adopted the cultural norms of spelling names when living for six generations on the planet, Copetrrea. My family is number 35. We will have good friends here. It's my family's responsibility to uphold what that means. That means we teach everyone what good friends means, and we provide a lot of examples and advice to make everyone follow the intention of a good friend. Am I talking too much?

3) **How old are you?** Age is sort of an odd concept you know there's this space-time age based on physicality, and then there's this biological age strain. Revolutions of Blue Origin around its star (the Sun) has always been the normal relationship on human-inhabited planets. By that standard, I'm twenty-three. Our planet has more density than Earth's and that makes our bio age slow because of the lower gravitational potential. Which makes me about twelve.

4) Are you gender-specific? Yes, sure. I'm all man.

5) Are you related to anyone in the story? Yes. I'm married to Danip, he's my husband and best friend. Marriage is a relationship on Planet 444. I think it is still a relationship on most planets. Maybe not. Actually, I'm not sure about that.

6) Where does your accent come from? Accent? What! I don't have an accent. Everyone adopted Space X English since we left Blue Origin to explore space. There's no accent. Well, wait. Vallena has a definite Hindu accent and the King has a distinct speaking style.

7) If you were to define one or two of the most crucial problems facing you, what are they and why? Crucial crunch time for getting some help from computer technology. Our work in soil conservation and plant nutritional value for a growing population on this land-disadvantaged planet has reached the end of our human ability. Humanoids wanted us to develop a social norm without technology-fueled greed and the destruction of natural resources that technology causes. But, we'll starve to death in three hundred years if we can't find solutions to the finite soil here.

8) What would a perfect world look like to you? Sweet candied walnuts, baby! We all get out of this Samsara trap and back to the source. Nobody knows what it look like because it isn't dis. But, that's the goal. Kung fu, is perfect.

9) What needs to happen to get from the problems to the perfect world you defined? I'm really hoping that between Mahá (The King) and Visákhá (The Queen) guiding our civilization to the intention of the Humanoid experiment, we will succeed. Everyone will have to do their part. Crucial this.

10) **If you weren't a character in this story who would you be in real life?** Everyone tells me I look like Fred The Godson. I'm arighwit it. He was poppin. Yeah, I could be dat.

11) **If you could change one thing about yourself, what would you change?** Hell no, you can't ask a man that. Wow. So what I would change bout me is to lose some of the extra weight. It's not healthy for my organs and frame to be this big. That's all though. Just the weight.

12) **What would you like to say to the reader?** Thanks, man! If it wasn't for you readers, I would be able to exist at all. If you would do me just one favor, baby. Tell the author to write more about me and my husband. We got some drama for you all. You need my story, y'all!

Contact Information

Join my mailing list to get a free story.

I seldom send you emails, and I never sell, share, or give your email address away.

[Signup Here and get a [1]**Free Story**[2]](

Please follow me on Twitter[3]. You can find me here. @markbertrand, https://twitter.com/markbertrand

Follow me on LinkedIn here[4]. https://www.linkedin.com/in/markbertrand/

Yes, I do have a Facebook, page here[5].

THANK YOU FOR ALL YOUR support and for buying my book!

Please give the book a five-star rating.

Other novels in this series: Starzel, The Dot, Love Reincarnate

---

1.   https://markbertrand.com/marks-newsletter-signup/

2.   **https://markbertrand.com/marks-newsletter-signup/**

3. https://twitter.com/markbertrand

4. https://www.linkedin.com/in/markbertrand/

5. https://www.facebook.com/Books-by-Mark-Bertrand-100246639255334

Don't miss out!

Visit the website below and you can sign up to receive emails whenever Mark Bertrand publishes a new book. There's no charge and no obligation.

https://books2read.com/r/B-A-UUSQ-ZNAUB

BOOKS 2 READ

Connecting independent readers to independent writers.

Also by Mark Bertrand

Nirvanaing
A Conscious Thing

Standalone
The Dot

Watch for more at https://markbertrand.com/.

www.ingramcontent.com/pod-product-compliance
Lightning Source LLC
Chambersburg PA
CBHW020118310726

48970CB00002B/689